THE TEN COMMANDMENTS

THE TEN COMMANDMENTS

Anthea Fraser

Chivers Press • Thorndike Press
Bath, England • Thorndike, Maine USA

This Large Print edition is published by Chivers Press, England, and by Thorndike Press, USA.

Published in 2000 in the U.K. by arrangement with HarperCollins Publishers.

Published in 2000 in the U.S. by arrangement with St. Martin's Press, LLC.

U.K. Hardcover   ISBN 0–7540–4070–4   (Chivers Large Print)
U.K. Softcover   ISBN 0–7540–4071–2   (Camden Large Print)
U.S. Softcover   ISBN 0–7862–2411–8   (General Series Edition)

The text of this Large Print edition is unabridged.
Other aspects of the book may vary from the original edition.

Set in 16 pt. New Times Roman.

Printed in Great Britain on acid-free paper.

British Library Cataloguing in Publication Data available

Library of Congress Cataloging-in-Publication Data

Fraser, Anthea.
      The ten commandments / Anthea Fraser.
         p.   cm.
      ISBN 0–7862–2411–8 (lg. print : sc : alk. paper)
      1. Webb, David (Fictitious character: Fraser)—Fiction.
      2. Villages—England—Fiction. 3. Police—England—Fiction.
      4. Large type books. I. Title.
      PR6056.R286 T45   2000b
      823'.914—dc21   99–087892

GREEN GROW THE RUSHES-O

I'll sing you one-O!
(Chorus) Green grow the rushes-O!
What is your one-O?
One is one and all alone and evermore shall be
so.

I'll sing you two-O!
(Chorus) Green grow the rushes-O!
What are your two-O?
Two, two, the lily-white Boys, clothed all in
green-O,
(Chorus) One is one and all alone and
evermore shall be so.

I'll sing you three-O!
(Chorus) Green grow the rushes-O!
What are your three-O?
Three, three, the Rivals,
(Chorus) Two, two, the lily-white Boys, clothed
all in green-O,
One is one and all alone and evermore shall be
so.

Four for the Gospel makers.
Five for the Symbols at your door.
Six for the six proud Walkers.
Seven for the seven Stars in the sky.
Eight for the April Rainers.
Nine for the nine bright Shiners.
Ten for the ten Commandments.
Eleven for the Eleven that went up to Heaven.
Twelve for the twelve Apostles.

CHAPTER ONE

The body lay sprawled face down between a Cortina and an Astra at the far end of the pub car park. In the warm darkness of the July evening, it was visible only if one glanced directly into the space between the vehicles.

'Who found him?' Detective Chief Inspector Webb asked the local police constable, who was preserving the scene.

'Driver of the Cortina, sir. Nearly fell over him, he said. Thought at first he'd just had one too many, till he looked closer.'

Webb grunted. He, too, had looked closer, noting the deep gash on the back of the head, the dark blood already clotting in the thick hair.

'Where is he?'

The constable jerked his head at the lighted pub behind them. 'In there, with the rest of them. The landlord had the sense to lock the doors as soon as the body was discovered.'

'I suppose that's something. We'll need to know if our friend here had been inside earlier, who he was with, etcetera. As soon as we can move him, we'll at least have a description to go on.'

He glanced irritably up at the new moon swinging in the sky. It afforded only the sketchiest illumination, and even that was masked by the bulk of the two cars.

'Where the hell are SOCO? Can't see a damn thing until we get some lights.'

Sergeant Jackson came up in time to hear his last comment. 'They've just arrived, Guv.'

Webb turned, to see the SOCO team making its way towards him between the rows of cars. He peered at his watch. It was just after eleven.

'Evening, Dave,' Dick Hodges greeted him. 'What have we got here?'

'You tell me, Dick. I can't see a bloody thing.'

'Stapleton been?'

'Not yet. I'll get out of your way—it's pretty cramped in there, and in any case, it's time I made a start on the statements.'

Hodges stood looking down at the body in its confined space. 'Ever had a sense of *déjà vu*?'

'It struck me, too. Five or six years ago, wasn't it?'

'That's right—a country pub, like this one. Bloke lying between two cars with his head bashed in. Far as I remember, the case was never cleared.'

'Thanks, Dick,' Webb said drily. 'Most encouraging.'

Hodges grinned and turned his attention to setting up the arc lights while Webb and Jackson walked across the car park to the pub entrance, guarded now by another uniformed constable.

'Nice-looking place,' Jackson said approvingly. 'Don't know it, do you, Guv?'

'I used to,' Webb replied, glancing up at the building as they approached. 'Matter of fact, I did my courting here. Looks as though it's changed a bit, though.'

In fact, he remembered as he went inside and stood blinking in the light, he'd been here more recently, on one ill-advised occasion with his ex-wife. Which, one way or another, had led to all sorts of trouble. He shook off the memories and surveyed the sea of faces turned towards him.

'DCI Webb,' he introduced himself as the landlord came round the bar to meet him, 'and this is Sergeant Jackson. Now, sir, what can you tell me about all this?'

'Absolutely nothing, Inspector.' The man was small and round, with sparse hair draped carefully over the crown of his head. 'First I knew was when Mr Caufield came running back to say someone had been hurt in the car park. We've had trouble before, so I told my barman to keep everyone inside, and hurried out to see what the form was. But—well, it was pretty obvious he was beyond help. I hope I did the right thing, detaining everyone?' This with an apologetic glance at his restive clientele.

'Indeed you did, Mr—?'

'Green—Charlie Green.'

3

'—Mr Green; you've saved us a lot of chasing around. Now, have you a snug or lounge bar which we can use to take statements?' He turned to the crowd of drinkers, avidly listening.

'A team of officers will be here shortly—we won't keep you any longer than necessary. In the meantime, perhaps I could start with the gentleman who found the body—Mr Caufield, was it?'

A man reluctantly detached himself from the throng. He was in his forties, of average height and—possibly because of his experience—very pale.

'I'm Bob Caufield.'

Webb nodded and, with Jackson and Caufield in his wake, followed the landlord to more private surroundings. The investigation had begun.

* * *

It was another two hours before Webb and Jackson were able to drive back to Shillingham. Things had taken their allotted course: the pathologist had duly arrived, and, to Webb's frustration if not his surprise, declined to commit himself as to whether or not death had occurred *in situ* or if the body'd been dumped later.

Extensive videos and still photographs had been taken, the outside of both cars dusted for

4

prints, and finally the body, securely wrapped in its bag, had been transported to the mortuary.

An unforeseen complication was that they still did not know its identity; the pockets had been stripped clean, leaving not so much as a handkerchief. Furthermore, the owner of the Astra had come forward and denied all knowledge of the victim, seeming to confirm that he'd no connection with either of the cars between which he'd been found. And finally, when the bar customers were at last allowed to leave, no car remained unclaimed. A series of negatives, Webb reflected glumly.

'Someone must have given him a lift,' Jackson opined, staring down the beam of his headlights. 'Stands to reason. There's nothing within five miles of the place.'

'So who was it? His murderer?'

'Must have been. No one else seems even to have *seen* him.'

'He wasn't particularly memorable, though, was he? After an evening's drinking in a crowded bar, would *you* remember a bloke of average height, mid forties, with fair hair and grey eyes? For a start, the description fits several of the men we've just seen.' He sighed. 'Still, once we get a photo circulated it might nudge someone's memory. On the other hand, it might not, if our lad never made it inside.'

'You think he was just driven there and promptly killed?'

'It's possible.'

'But why? If Chummie wanted to clobber him, there are more secluded spots to do it than a pub car park. Anyone could have come along.'

'Suppose they *were* going for a drink, but had a row on the way there? Hang on, let's work out the timing; the Astra driver says he arrived about eight-thirty, and the driver of the Cortina, Caufield, just before nine, taking the last space in the car park. He couldn't have helped seeing the body if it had been there—in fact, he'd have stepped on it as he got out of the car.'

'So if he took the last place, where did the killer park?'

'Someone must have left in the meantime.'

'Mind you,' Jackson went on, 'it mightn't have been the bloke he came with who did for him. Suppose someone came weaving out of the pub, and our lad, who'd just arrived, told him he wasn't fit to drive? Chummie, aggressively drunk, biffs him over the head and drives off and the victim's pal, not wanting to be involved, also scarpers?'

'Not a very friendly act, but surely he'd have made at least an anonymous call before now? And who went through the pockets? Still, I agree the thing's wide open. We've got the names of several people who left during the crucial period—perhaps they'll throw some light on it. Lord knows we could do with it; all we've got at the moment is victim—unknown, killer—unknown, motive—possibly robbery, but that could be a red herring. Time of death between nine and ten-thirty, and that's about it.'

'Never mind, Guv, most likely his wife will have reported him missing by the morning.' Jackson glanced at Webb's impassive face. 'Think there could be a connection with the Feathers case? I heard DI Hodges mention it.'

'There are similarities, certainly. I'll get out the file on it tomorrow.'

Jackson drew up outside Webb's gate and leaned across him to open the door.

'Thanks, Ken. See you in the morning—or rather, later today.' Wearily, Webb climbed out of the car and set off up the gravelled drive of what had once been a gracious old house, to the four-square block of flats which now stood there and which he regarded as home.

* * *

Hannah James opened her eyes and stretched luxuriously. School had broken up last Friday for the long summer holidays, and there was no hurry to get out of bed. Furthermore, it wasn't only the term that had ended, but her year in charge while Gwen Rutherford, the headmistress, had been on sabbatical in Canada. For today, Gwen was coming home.

Hannah watched the curtains rise and fall in

7

the breeze from the window. She'd be glad to see her again—of course she would. They were not only colleagues but friends of long-standing—since, in fact, they'd been schoolgirls themselves at Ashbourne—and their joint authority as head and deputy had worked very well. Nevertheless, and to her shame, Hannah was aware of a niggle of resentment that she would no longer be in charge, would have to abdicate her authority and revert to second-in-command.

Though obviously she'd said nothing, David, bless him, had seemed to understand. He'd asked her, last night, if she'd any reservations about Gwen's return, but before she could answer he'd been called out to a suspicious death. Par for the course, she thought with a smile.

She tucked the pillow under her chin, and let her mind drift back over their relationship. They'd met seven years ago, when Gwen had called in the police over a spate of anonymous letters at school. At that time, David had been divorced for two years and was living in cramped lodgings the other side of Shillingham. During the course of the investigation, he'd mentioned that he was looking for somewhere of his own, and, after considerable thought, Hannah mentioned the vacant flat at the top of her own building.

It had been a calculated risk, since his proximity would necessarily mean they'd see

8

more of each other. There was already an attraction between them, but her career was of paramount importance, and she could not afford gossip. Nor had she had any wish to become entangled in a situation that would make demands on her, and marriage had no place in her plans. It had been an enormous relief to discover that David felt the same. Once bitten, twice shy, she supposed, recalling her brief meeting with his ex-wife.

Their relationship had blossomed, with the added piquancy that not even their closest friends knew of it—a secret easy to maintain since they lived in the same building. They remained essentially free spirits—though there had been occasional flares of jealousy on both sides—and often met simply as friends. But on the occasions when they made love, they experienced a sense of fulfilment that neither had found elsewhere. Which, Hannah concluded humbly, made them both very lucky.

She glanced at the bedside clock. Eight-thirty, she saw, with a stab of guilt. Gwen, who was returning on the overnight flight, would probably already have left Heathrow, which meant she'd be home in less than two hours. Hannah had left a note offering to take round a cold supper, to save her friend having to dash out and shop as soon as she reached home. Gwen would, she knew, be anxious to hear about Ashbourne and how it had fared in her absence.

Hannah sighed. Then she swung her legs to the floor and padded through to the bathroom.

*   *   *

Gwen Rutherford was not the only Broadshire resident returning on the Toronto flight; Frederick Mace and his wife had spent a month in Canada promoting his book on criminality, and as the plane touched down, the knowledge that he would shortly be home filled him with relief. It had been an exhausting tour for a couple in their seventies, added to which the dreaded cloud of jet lag now hung over them.

He put his hand on Edwina's. 'All right, darling?'

She turned to smile at him. 'All right, but I'll be glad to be home.'

'My sentiments exactly. Not long now; one of the girls will be waiting for us.'

It was Gillian, Edwina saw, as she emerged from the customs hall to scan the row of people meeting the flight. She smiled and waved as she hurried after Frederick and the luggage-laden trolley.

'Darlings!' Gillian embraced them enthusiastically. 'Did you have a wonderful time? How many books did you sign, Pop?'

He smiled, his face crinkling into all the

folds that made him so distinctively himself. 'I lost count,' he confessed.

'He was a great success,' Edwina said proudly. 'And how are all of you?'

'Fine, and steaming in this wonderful hot weather.'

'And Alex?'

Gillian didn't meet her eyes. 'Fine,' she said again, brightly. 'The twins broke up last week, so her life has swung into holiday mode.'

They located the car and loaded cases, holdalls and carrier bags into the boot. Already the concrete building was uncomfortably hot.

'You get in the front, dear, so you can tell Gilly about the trip,' Edwina instructed her husband, opening the rear door. 'I shall probably have a little nap on the way home.'

'Was it as disruptive as you'd feared,' Gillian asked, manoeuvring the car down the ramps, 'having to break off in the middle of the new book to talk about the last one?'

'I tried to keep it fresh in my mind—jotting down ideas, and so on. I'll be glad to get back to it, though.'

'Didn't you say it's about the motives behind crimes?'

'That's the general idea.' Gillian smiled wryly, accepting that further questioning would be useless; her father would never discuss work in progress. 'There was a murder near Shillingham last night,' she remarked instead. 'It was on local radio. And talking of the media, I hope you've not forgotten your TV interview in all the excitement?'

'No, but I'm looking forward to a few good nights' sleep before I have to face that. At the moment I'm having trouble in stringing two sentences together.'

Their voices, distorted by the noise of the engine, came and went against Edwina's ears, making little sense. Gilly looked well, she thought fondly, her blonde hair streaked by the sun and her skin bronzed and glowing. She'd hardly changed in appearance since she was sixteen, and it was difficult to remember she had a sixteen-year-old daughter of her own. At least one of her children was happily married, Edwina thought, and the dormant anxiety about Alex reared itself again. She and Roy were going through a difficult time and there was no knowing how it would end.

And on the familiar worry her tired eyelids drooped and she slept.

*　　*　　*

Before attending the postmortem that morning, Webb had driven out to Force Headquarters at Stonebridge, where the files of uncleared cases were kept in the basement. He'd spent some time going through that relating to the Feathers case, making notes and learning additional details in the process.

12

Trevor Philpott, aged forty-four, had been killed by a blow to the back of the head on the ninth of November six years ago. His body was discovered between two parked cars behind the Feathers pub off the Erlesborough to Oxbury road, a location, as Dick Hodges had commented, very similar to last night's. However, it had not in fact been the scene of the crime, traces of blood having been found in a field just beyond the car park.

Despite widespread investigations, no one had been apprehended, no motive discovered, and all inquiries had drawn a blank. Philpott had, to all appearances, been in the best of health, happily married, with a good job and no financial worries. Apparent end of story.

Several hours later, and with the postmortem behind him, Webb was sitting at his desk reading through his notes when the phone rang. He reached for it without looking up. 'Webb.'

'Morning, Dave. Harry Good, in Ashmartin.'

'Hello, Harry. What can I do for you?'

'Boot's on the other foot, old lad. I think we can supply a name for your body.'

Webb straightened. 'Oh? Someone reported missing?'

'Yep, one Simon Judd, a social worker. I haven't any details yet, but according to his wife he arranged to meet someone for a drink last night and never came home.'

13

'Do we know who?'

'Bloke called Jim Fairlie, for what it's worth. Judd doesn't seem to have known him—took him for a new client. Anyway, he rang Judd at work, and they arranged to meet outside the Jester on Dominion Street at nine o'clock.'

'That's a long way from the Nutmeg.'

'That's what she's clinging to, poor woman, but the description ties in. He left home about ten to nine, and that was the last she saw of him.'

'Did he take a car?'

'No, they're only ten minutes' walk from the town centre.'

Webb said thoughtfully, 'Remember the Feathers case, Harry?'

'No, when was that?'

'It'll be six years now, come November.'

'I was still with Gloucestershire then.'

'Well, see how this grabs you. An estate agent, one Trevor Philpott, received a phone call from someone claiming to have a house to sell. The man offered to drive him out to value it, since the place was difficult to find. They met outside the Stag at Oxbury, and, some hours later, Philpott's body was found between two cars behind another pub, the Feathers, off the Erlesborough road.'

'Good God, that's quite a coincidence.'

'Or perhaps not; the murderer's still on the loose.'

Good whistled softly. 'The pub killer strikes

again?'

'Could be. There's another point that tallies: I'm just back from the PM, and death did not occur *in situ*. He was dumped afterwards—and so was Trevor Philpott.'

'Good God!' Good said again, with even more emphasis.

'Erlesborough handled the last case, but I've been through the file and there's very little to go on. No evidence of any kind and no apparent motive.'

'Doesn't bode too well, does it? Anyway, to come back to this one, we're about to bring Mrs Judd over to identify the body, if that's OK?'

'Yes, he's been tidied up. I'll be glad of a talk with her, if she's up to it.'

'She should be OK, her brother and sister-in-law will be with her. We should be there in about half an hour.'

'Right, I'll meet you at the mortuary.'

'And perhaps, when the formalities are over, we can get together over a pint?'

'You're on. See you then.'

*　　*　　*

However, when, an hour or so later, Webb and Good settled down in the Brown Bear to pool their knowledge, they had little further to add. Mrs Judd, pale and trembling, had identified the body as that of her husband. Under

15

Webb's gentle questioning, she tearfully insisted that he'd no enemies, had not quarrelled with anyone, had not seemed under any kind of strain. It was the Philpott case all over again.

They finished their lunch in gloomy silence. 'We've got two house-to-house inquiries under way,' Good said eventually, finishing his beer. 'One in the area around his home and one in the town centre, on the off chance that someone saw them meet. God knows what happened after that. Our lads will be in the Jester this evening to speak to the regulars, but two blokes talking in a pub wouldn't have made that much of an impression.'

'Perhaps,' Webb suggested, 'the Jester was only a rendezvous—you know, "on the corner at nine". Then Chummie draws up in his car and says, "It's a lovely evening—let's drive out and find a country pub."'

'Bit hypothetical, isn't it?'

'Have you any better suggestion? Assuming the murder was premeditated, he'd have wanted to get Judd out of town to do the dirty deed, and he must have had a car to get to the Nutmeg. We know Judd hadn't taken his.'

Good pushed back his plate. 'OK, Dave, it's your baby now. Anything I can do, you've only to say the word. I've arranged for half a dozen DCs and DSs to report to the Incident Room. They might be able to help.'

'Thanks, Harry. I'll be following you over

shortly; the first priority is to interview Judd's colleagues and see what they know about that phone call. I'm determined this case isn't going to fizzle out like the Philpott one.'

'That's right, think positively,' Good said with a grin. 'With a bit of luck, you might finish by cracking both of them.'

*   *   *

Ashmartin lay to the east, near the Berkshire border. It was a charming old town which had expanded over the years to become the third largest in the county. In the process, however, it had had the wisdom—or good fortune—to retain its nucleus of attractive old buildings, the responsibility for which had, over the last thirty years, been in the hands of a vigilant preservation society.

To Webb's mind, a large part of the town's charm lay in its centre, for the parish church of St Giles, resplendent with towers and turrets, overlooked a large green complete with duck pond—another legacy from the past. Here, in the summer, office workers picnicked, children played, and older inhabitants sat in the shade under spreading trees.

Several private houses also overlooked the green, and in fact, as Good had indicated, most of the residential areas were within walking distance of the centre. Consequently, Ashmartin was spared the nightly migration of

17

its population suffered by most town centres.

And as if these blessings were not enough, it was here that the Broadshire and Avon Canal began its winding journey westwards across the county, affording pleasant walks and interesting pubs along its banks.

'This is where I'm coming when I retire,' Jackson remarked. 'You can keep your south coast—Ashmartin's the place for me.'

'You could do a lot worse, Ken. Look, there's a space here. Pull in, and we can walk round the corner to Social Services.'

The heat of the afternoon hit them as soon as they left the car, beating up from the pavement and down from the molten blue sky, and they were thankful to turn into the shady side street, screened from the sun by its tall buildings.

The Social Services Department was halfway along, and Webb pushed open the door to find himself in a foyer not unlike a doctor's surgery. To the right was a children's play area, where much shrieking and banging was in progress, and a few dispirited women—presumably the children's mothers—sat patiently round the room flicking through magazines.

He took out his warrant card and approached the desk, raising his voice to make himself heard. 'DCI Webb and Sergeant Jackson, from Shillingham. We'd like to speak to someone about Mr Judd.'

The young woman bit her lip. 'Yes, of course. We just can't believe—' She broke off. 'Just a moment, I'll see if the duty officer is free.'

She lifted the intercom and spoke quickly in a low voice, then turned back to them. 'He'll come straight down, sir.'

'Thank you.'

One of the doors on the left opened to discharge a young couple, shepherded by an older man who stopped on the threshold and shook their hands. Interview rooms, Webb thought, much as they had at Carrington Street. He turned as footsteps sounded on the stairs and a dark, bearded man hurried towards them.

'Chief Inspector—Steve Parker, one of Simon's colleagues. As you can imagine, we're all shattered. Would you care to come up to my office?'

Webb and Jackson followed him back up the linoleumed stairs and into a room shaded by venetian blinds, where an electric fan whirred officiously in a corner. There were two desks, one of them poignantly bare. Parker seated himself at the other and waved them to a couple of chairs.

He said in a strained voice, 'I suppose there's no chance of a mistake?'

'I'm afraid not; his wife identified him this afternoon.'

'God!' Parker put his elbows on the desk

19

and his head in his hands. After a moment, he raised his head and met Webb's eye. 'He broke all the rules, you know, going off alone to meet someone.'

'Then why did he do it?'

Parker shrugged. 'I was here when the call came through; I—'

'Just a moment, sir—about that call: was it for Mr Judd specifically, or did he just happen to be free?'

'I checked with Diane downstairs; she said he was asked for by name.'

So it wasn't a random killing—always supposing that the caller was the murderer. 'It would be a help if you could remember what was said.'

'I've been over and over it, but you see the phone was for ever ringing, and to begin with I didn't pay much attention. The first thing I registered was Simon saying, "I'm sorry, I can't place you. When was that?" But I really pricked up my ears when he said, "I think it would be much better if you came here. We can speak quite privately."

'The other bloke was obviously arguing, and I made signs to Simon asking what was up, but he just shook his head. He finished by saying, "Well, all right then, if you really think that's best. Yes, I'll be there. Nine o'clock outside the Jester."

'I said quickly, "Simon, you know you can't—" but he'd already put down the phone.'

'And the caller gave the name of Jim Fairlie?'

'That's right. It didn't ring a bell with Simon, but the man said they'd met a few years ago. He rattled off names of supposedly mutual friends, though Si didn't recognize any of them. Anyway, he'd got some problem, and suggested discussing it over a pint.'

'Why wouldn't he come here?'

'Said his wife worked in an office across the street, and he didn't want her to see him. I think Si finally gave in because of the alleged social connection.'

'Even though he didn't remember the man, or any of the names he'd mentioned?'

Parker gave a wry smile. 'That was nothing unusual; old Simon was famous for his bad memory. It caused him endless embarrassment, and he'd pretend to remember people, even if he didn't, to avoid hurting their feelings. Anyway, I did my best to stop him going, though I knew it was hopeless; you can't let a client down once an appointment's made, and he'd no way of contacting Fairlie. So I told him I'd go with him, but he laughed and said, "Stop fussing, Steve, it'll be OK. Anyway, he might clam up if there are two of us, and I'm only going for a drink, for God's sake."'

Parker stopped speaking, and in the silence noises floated up from the street through the open window and the fan whirred relentlessly.

21

Webb said, 'Did he make any comment about the man's voice, how he sounded?'

'He said he seemed on edge.'

It wasn't much to go on. 'Well, we'll do our best to trace him.' Privately, Webb feared Fairlie would prove as elusive as Philpott's bogus house vendor. He went over to the window and separated two slats of the blind to peer across the street. 'What offices are over there?'

'Solicitors, patent agents, accountants—you name it.'

'We'll get a team on to it, see if there's a Mrs Fairlie working in any of them. Not,' he added heavily, 'that I'll be holding my breath.'

'He *might* have given his own name,' Parker said desperately, 'if he hadn't actually planned to kill Simon.'

'Possibly.' Webb nodded to Jackson, who put away his notebook and stood up. 'You can't think of any client Mr Judd had an altercation with? Anyone who might have harboured a grudge?'

'No, he was a placid chap, dedicated to the job. He didn't let anyone rile him; in fact, the rest of us used to call him in to calm things down if tempers got frayed.'

'Well, thank you, Mr Parker. Get in touch if you think of anything else, however unimportant it seems.'

Parker saw them to his door and they went in silence down the stairs. Webb walked over to the reception desk.

'Did anything strike you, miss, about the caller who phoned Mr Judd yesterday?'

She blinked back tears. 'His voice was shaking—he sounded upset.' She looked up at him. 'That's not unusual, though. We get all sorts ringing in.'

'Was it a young voice, would you say?'

'It was hard to tell, with the shaking. Not *old*, anyway.'

'Accent?'

'Local, I think.'

'And he asked for Mr Judd by name; what were his exact words?'

' "Is Mr Judd there? It's very important that I speak to him." '

'That was all?'

'Yes. So I—put him through.'

Webb nodded. 'Thank you.' He turned on his heel and, with Jackson beside him, strode through the noisy reception area out into the street.

CHAPTER TWO

Hannah felt oddly nervous as she stood on Gwen's doorstep and pressed the bell. It was eleven months since they'd seen each other, and a lot had happened to both of them.

It was still warm; the sun was low in the sky,

bathing the park behind her with its rich light. A game of tennis was in progress, and the plop of balls and the occasional call of 'Out!' reached her as she waited.

Then the door opened and Gwen stood there, squinting in the sunlight which gilded her face—Gwen, just as she'd always been, with her tall, gawky frame and the strands of hair escaping from their French pleat to curl endearingly on her neck.

'Hannah! You're a gem to do this! How lovely to see you!' She clasped Hannah awkwardly to her, endangering the basket of food which she held.

'Welcome home, Gwen! What a long time it's been!'

'Come in. Isn't it hot? Just like a Canadian summer.'

They went together into the little hall, dark-seeming after the evening light outside, and, by tacit agreement, made for the kitchen. The table-top was almost invisible under a pile of mail and free newspapers, and Hannah perforce laid her basket on a counter.

'I'm afraid there's rather an odd smell,' Gwen said apologetically, 'due, I suppose, to the house being shut up for so long, though Beatrice did come in to air it.' She shot Hannah a glance. 'She tells me you've seen quite a bit of each other over the last twelve months.'

'We—met at various functions.'

24

'And also on less congenial occasions?'

But Hannah was not yet ready to discuss the deaths of a member of staff and a school governor during Gwen's absence, both in distressing circumstances.

'I'll put the wine and food in the fridge, shall I, till we're ready for them? It's salad—I didn't think you'd want anything hot on an evening like this.'

'No, indeed, and your salads are so special. Unlike mine, which, as you know to your cost, are simply bits of lettuce and tomato thrown on to a plate.'

'Have you seen your mother yet?' Hannah asked, disconcertingly aware of the need to make conversation.

'No, I was shattered when I got home and went straight to bed. I spoke to her on the phone, though. Bea suggested not bringing her back till tomorrow, to give me time to settle in.'

Old Mrs Rutherford had lived with Gwen for as long as Hannah could remember—or perhaps it was Gwen who lived with her. During the sabbatical, she had stayed with her elder daughter and son-in-law. Hannah gathered from John Templeton, who was also the school doctor, that the old lady's eyesight was troublesome, and wondered anxiously how that would affect Gwen.

'I thought we might have a drink on the terrace,' Gwen was continuing. 'It's still warm, though the sun's moved off it.'

'That'd be lovely.'

'What will you have? Duty-free gin and tonic?'

'Sounds perfect.'

Hannah watched her pour the drinks, splashing tonic water over the mail in a typically 'Gwen' fashion. She never failed to marvel that this gauche woman with the diffident brown eyes was in reality a brilliant academic with a will of iron. Many was the parent, Hannah reflected, who, to his cost, had underestimated the headmistress of Ashbourne School for Girls.

'You carry the glasses—I'd only spill them—and I'll go ahead and open doors.'

They walked back into the hall and through the familiar sitting-room, which, as Gwen had said, did smell a trifle musty. She bent to unbolt the old-fashioned French windows and pushed them wide. Out on the narrow stone terrace was a wooden bench and a rickety iron table which, to Hannah's mind, could have done with a good scrub. No doubt at least a year's grime coated it, but Gwen didn't seem to notice. She sank down on the bench with a sigh, stretching out her long legs.

'Home sweet home!'

'Are you glad to be back?' Hannah asked her.

'Oh, I think so, though I hated leaving Canada.'

'From your letters, you seemed to have a busy social life.'

'Yes, there was always something going on.'

'And you liked the school?' Hannah prompted.

'It was excellent; I'm hoping to adapt some of their ideas for Ashbourne. We must discuss them as soon as we have a moment.'

There was a pause. Hannah said, 'Thank you for going to see my parents.' They had emigrated to Canada twenty years previously.

'It was a pleasure, especially to find them so well. They wanted to hear every last detail about you.'

'But they already know it! I write regularly and we speak on the phone at least once a month.'

'Well, they still had plenty of questions.' A sly, sideways look. 'They wanted to know if you had a "young man".'

Hannah smiled. 'And what did you say?'

'That if you had, you were keeping him to yourself.' She added gently, 'They want grandchildren, Hannah, and you're their only chance.'

'A pretty slim one, by now.'

Gwen reached for her glass and stared thoughtfully into it. 'Do you ever feel you're missing out, not being married?'

Hannah raised her eyebrows. 'No; do you?'

Though they'd been at school together, Gwen was in fact five years Hannah's senior, a

27

prefect when she herself was in the first form. To Hannah's knowledge, there had never been a man in her life; but then, she reminded herself, Gwen knew nothing of David. Close though their friendship had been, there was an unspoken ban on discussing intimate subjects, and Gwen's question now had taken her by surprise. She was even more surprised that Gwen hadn't immediately answered hers.

'Do you, Gwen?' she repeated, turning to face her.

Gwen was staring dreamily down the length of the garden. 'A year ago, I'd have said of course not. Now, I'm not so sure.'

'Don't tell me you've fallen for a Mountie!' Hannah teased, and was amazed to see her friend flush.

'Take no notice,' Gwen said quickly. 'I'm getting maudlin in my old age. Now, I want to hear all about Ashbourne.'

So, since the moment could no longer be delayed, Hannah took another sip of her drink and began her report.

*   *   *

'Darling?'

Gillian Coburn looked up from her easel as her husband's voice reached her from two flights below.

'In the studio,' she called.

She met him in the doorway, his jacket

28

slung over one shoulder and his tie loosened.

'Sorry, love, I didn't hear the car.'

'Deaf to all else when the muse strikes, eh?' He kissed her. 'Did you meet the plane all right?'

'Yes, it was on time, thank goodness.'

'How are your parents?'

'Exhausted, poor loves, but they'll soon bounce back. The tour seems to have been a great success. Not only that, Pop's making strides with the new book, too.'

'I hope I have as much energy at his age.' He paused, his eyes on her face. 'Did they ask about Alex?'

'Of course.'

'What did you say?'

'As little as possible. They'll see for themselves soon enough.'

'I wish there was something we could do,' Hugh said worriedly. 'It's grim having to sit on the sidelines while they destroy each other. Can't you talk to her?'

'I've tried, but you know Alex; she can be very prickly, specially when she's unhappy.'

'She wasn't at the house to meet them?'

'No, she'd arranged to take the twins to London today; they wanted to go round the Tower.'

'In this heat? She's a saint.'

'She said she'd ring them when she gets back, and call round tomorrow.'

Hugh moved past her and stood looking at

29

the painting on the easel. Gillian was making quite a name for herself as an illustrator of children's books, and, an architect himself, he was fascinated by the way she built up a picture.

'It's coming along well, isn't it? Are you pleased with it?'

'Fairly; I'm not quite happy with the little boy. He's a complex character for a children's story, and I don't think I've got him quite right.'

She came to stand beside him, frowning slightly, until the slamming of the front door broke their concentration.

'Hello?' came their daughter's voice. 'I'm home! Where is everybody?'

Hugh and Gillian exchanged a smile. 'Coming!' they called back, and, with Hugh's arm round his wife's shoulder, they went together down the stairs.

*   *   *

Unusually, Hannah arrived back at Beechcroft Mansions at the same time as Webb, and waited while he garaged his car.

'You're working late,' she greeted him. 'Is this the case you were called to last night?'

'Yes; it's been the hell of a day, I can tell you—the PM, interviewing the widow, then over to Ashmartin. I was there till after seven, since when I've been in the Incident Room.'

'Why Ashmartin, for heaven's sake?'

'Because that's where the victim came from. He was a social worker, and on the face of it, it looks as though one of his clients turned nasty.'

'On the face of it?'

'Well, it's more complicated than that. In fact, it's very similar to a case we had some years ago, which is still on file.'

The church clock was chiming ten as they went into the building. 'I hope you've eaten?' Hannah said.

He nodded. 'One of the lads brought in pizzas. And you, I take it, have been to Gwen's?'

'Yes; she was pretty tired, so I left soon after we'd eaten.'

'And you survived the grilling on your stewardship?'

'Just about. Of course, she knew the worst of it already; John and I had both sent her full reports, so it was just a rehash.'

'Well, you must admit you had an eventful year.'

The lift stopped at Hannah's floor. 'Like to come in for a nightcap?'

'Love to,' he said with alacrity.

Hannah's flat always seemed a haven after a difficult day, its soothing pastels and relaxing atmosphere a balm to the soul. Tonight, despite the still-oppressive heat outdoors, it felt pleasantly cool. He sidestepped the marmalade cat which came to greet them, winding itself round Hannah's legs with a mew half-welcome, half-complaint.

'I know, I know,' she told it, 'you're starving, as usual. Come along, then, and I'll give you some biscuits.'

Webb leaned against the kitchen door, watching her. 'Has Canada changed Gwen at all, or is she as scatty as ever?'

Hannah paused, the packet of cat food in her hand. 'I'm not sure. She's *not* quite the same, but it's nothing I can put my finger on. Perhaps we've just forgotten some of each other's foibles.'

She shook the packet into the cat's bowl. 'What *does* worry me is that she's bent on introducing some Canadian methods to Ashbourne, and I'm not sure I like the sound of that.'

'It's just the first flush of enthusiasm,' Webb said comfortably. 'Once she settles back into the old routine, she'll probably opt for laissez faire.'

Hannah took the ice-tray from the fridge and moved past him to the sitting-room. 'Actually,' she admitted, taking two glasses out of the cabinet, 'I've introduced a few changes myself while she's been away. Nothing drastic, but they've made things run more smoothly.'

Webb laughed. 'By the sound of it, you'll have to do some bargaining. "You can do that, if I can keep this."'

'Except that she's the boss again now.' She carried the drinks to the coffee table and they sat down in the deep, comfortable chairs.

'Anyway, enough of that; we must wait and see.' She sipped her drink and leant back, resting her head against the cushions. 'I love summer evenings,' she said, 'when the heat of the day is over and you can relax and draw breath, and everything's so peaceful.'

'Amen to that.' He raised his glass. 'To peace and tranquillity!'

Hannah laughed. 'Put like that, it sounds rather dull.' She watched him for a moment. 'You're still thinking about the case, aren't you?'

'Sorry.'

'Want to talk it over?'

He sighed. 'No, love, never mind, I'll keep it to myself for the moment. Perhaps when I've slept on it, some chink of light might appear.'

*   *   *

It wasn't until the next morning that Frederick Mace read about the murder, and, with a mounting sense of excitement, realized its personal significance.

'Good God!' he exclaimed at the breakfast table.

His wife moved the marmalade out of range of his paper. 'What is it, dear?'

'This murder that Gillian mentioned: it

sounds like a replica of one I selected for my book.'

'It shouldn't take long to clear up, then,' Edwina commented.

'Unfortunately that doesn't follow; I think I told you I'd decided to include one unsolved crime? Well, that was it. I hoped, by working out possible motives, to come up with a new angle.'

'And did you?' she asked, refilling his coffee cup.

'I haven't started on it yet; all I've done is gather in the facts. But the press are speculating that this latest murder might be connected with it. You see, in both cases, the victim—a man in his forties—was found in a pub car park, bashed over the head.'

'Good gracious,' Edwina said mildly.

Frederick pushed back his chair. 'Excuse me, dear, I must catch Paul before he leaves the house.'

Paul Blake was a part-time librarian, part-time researcher, and part-time secretary to Frederick—which, as he sometimes remarked, meant that he frequently worked overtime.

To Frederick's relief, he answered the phone immediately. 'Mr Mace! I was just about to ring you.'

'About the pub murder?'

'Yes, I see they're comparing it with the Feathers case.'

'Which,' Frederick reminded him drily, 'you

tried to dissuade me from looking into.'

'I didn't want us attracting the murderer's attention. Come to that, I still don't.'

'Well, despite your qualms, you came up with some useful details, but I haven't had time even to glance at them. Are you rushing out, or could you give me a quick run-through?'

There was a smile in Blake's voice. 'As you know, sir, I'm pretty flexible.'

'Excellent. Then perhaps you'd refresh my memory—after a month away, I've forgotten the details.'

Blake did so, summarizing the known facts and the lack of official progress.

Frederick grunted. 'Um. We didn't make contact with the widow, did we?'

'No, she'd remarried and moved away.'

'But as far as we know, her first marriage was a happy one?'

'According to all reports, yes.'

'I wonder, though. I might be quite wrong, but when I first saw his photograph, Philpott reminded me of someone I once knew—chap called Roger Denby, who was a real ladies' man. It was something about the mouth and those heavy-lidded eyes.'

'Well, the police didn't unearth anything, and their inquiries were more detailed than mine.'

'Ah, but they hadn't the advantage of knowing Denby,' Frederick said.

Blake laughed. 'All right, sir, I'll make some more inquiries and see what I come up with. How did the tour go?'

'Very well, as far as I could judge. I'll tell you about it when I see you. There are a few notes to type up, too. However, my first priority is to prepare for the television interview. It's being recorded on Thursday.'

'Lord, yes—I'd forgotten. And going out on Friday, isn't it?'

'That's right, on this new Arts programme. And as soon as that's over—next Tuesday, to be exact—the local library has asked me to give a talk as part of their Festival of Literature. Which, as you'll appreciate, doesn't leave much time for writing during the next week or so.'

'Well, good luck anyway. Shall I come and collect the notes?'

'There's no hurry; it'll do when you call in with your findings.'

'If any,' Blake said.

'I have the greatest faith in you, Paul.' Frederick put down the phone, the words still echoing in his head, and acknowledged to himself they were no more than the truth. Paul Blake had made himself invaluable in a remarkably short space of time, someone who could be depended on to do whatever was asked of him.

He sat back, allowing his gaze to wander through the study window, and was reminded of Edwina's comment when, all those years ago, he had positioned his desk immediately in front of it.

'You'll never get any work done if you sit there—it's far too distracting!'

For Brighton Villa was right in the centre of Ashmartin, overlooking both the green and the frontage of St Giles's church. There was always something to watch from its windows, and, sitting at his desk, Frederick felt he had his finger on the pulse of the town.

The villa itself was a protected building, a tall, narrow house, graciously proportioned and standing on arguably the most desirable site in town. It had a small garden at the front and a slightly larger one at the rear, secluded by trees and a high wall from curious eyes.

On this warm July morning, people were pouring across the green on their way to work, the women in brightly coloured dresses, the men as informally attired as their offices permitted. Across the green, a delivery wagon had pulled up to offload barrels of beer at the Jester public house.

Frederick's brows drew together in a frown. It was outside the Jester, apparently, that the victim and his killer had met. Frustrating to reflect that had it taken place a day later, he might himself have witnessed their meeting. Not, of course, that it would have meant anything to him at the time.

The phone on his desk rang, making him

jump. 'Frederick Mace,' he said into it.

'Pop! How are you? Welcome back!'

'Alex!' The murders faded from his mind, giving way to a wave of affection and anxiety for his younger daughter. 'I hear you're coming over today?'

'That's why I'm phoning; I wasn't sure what time the twins' tennis coaching was, but it's this morning. So will this afternoon be OK, about three?'

'Whenever you like; we'll be here.'

'See you then. 'Bye.' She rang off.

Frederick replaced the phone thoughtfully. Though he'd be pleased, of course, to see his grandsons, their presence would preclude the chance of a proper talk with Alex. Which, perhaps, was exactly what she intended.

*   *   *

As they drove through fields of ripening corn on their way to Erlesborough, Webb was in reflective mood. It was exactly a year since the town had featured so largely and so traumatically in his investigations, a case which had involved digging deeply into his own family history. Well, that was water under the bridge now, and at least the result had been a closer relationship with his sister. Not that he'd have time to contact her today.

He had decided that before he made any further inquiries on the Judd case, he needed to satisfy himself as to exactly how close the parallels were with the previous one. And the man to help him with that was the officer who had been in charge of it, DCI Ted Ferris.

They were approaching the familiar bend which led into the town; and Webb mentally braced himself, as always when visiting the place of his youth. The memories were still not happy, even if the worst of them had been expunged.

'You remember the way to the nick, no doubt,' he observed. Jackson merely nodded, knowing the governor to be touchy when in this vicinity. The pavements were crowded with market stalls and he almost missed the turning into Silver Street, a short, cobbled cul-de-sac where the police station was situated. He turned up the narrow alleyway alongside the building to the parking area at the back, and they got out of the car in silence and walked round to the front of the station.

Ted Ferris was of medium height and rather more than medium weight, with a cheerful, rosy face and thinning hair.

'Dave!' he exclaimed, when a DC showed them into his office. 'Long time no see!' He came round his desk with his hand outstretched, and Webb took it.

'How are you, Ted? We missed you last year—on a course, weren't you?'

'Right; Mick Charlton filled me in. Bad business all round.'

39

'Well,' Webb said briskly, 'you know what I've come about this time.' He sat down as Ferris waved him and Jackson to a couple of chairs.

'To remind me of my failings, no doubt. These uncleared cases are the very devil.'

'Perhaps we can sort it for you. As you know, we've been landed with almost a carbon copy. If we work in harness, we might come up with something.'

'Fine by me. What do you want to know?'

'Everything you've got, really. I've been through the files at Stonebridge, but it's all pretty cut and dried. What I want is the human element, feelings—suspicions, even—that were not strong enough to be noted officially. Suppose you go through it from the beginning, so we can compare the cases step by step?'

Ferris sat back, rubbing a hand over his face. 'To be honest, I can't see what the hell more we could have done. Anyway, judge for yourself.

'As you know, it was nearly six years ago. The first we knew about it was when we got a call from the Feathers's landlord around closing time, to report a body being found in the car park. I went out there myself. No one in the pub recognized the man's description— or wouldn't let on if they did. But since he lived in Oxbury, it wouldn't have been his local anyway.'

'Go on.'

'We discovered later that he was killed just outside a pedestrian entrance at the back of the car park. SOCO found traces of blood on the grass, and signs of a body being dragged through the opening. Fibres matched the victim's clothes.'

'So possibly the only connection with the pub was as a dumping ground?'

'That's what it looked like, though God knows why he wasn't left where he was. Other than that, we came up with damn-all—no fingerprints, no foot marks, nothing. As for the victim, we were assured he was in good health, and had a steady job, an adequate bank balance, and a loving wife. Too good to be true.'

'Perhaps it was,' Webb suggested.

Ferris flashed him a look. 'If he was leading a double life, he took it with him to the grave. We grilled everyone who'd had any contact with him, but nothing emerged that we could get our teeth into.'

'Hobbies?'

'Sport, mainly football and cricket. Used to play for Oxbury United in his heyday, and still turned out for the first eleven every summer.'

'One of the lads, then?'

'I suppose so.'

'What was his wife like?'

'Small, quite pretty. Not a lot to say for herself, but we didn't exactly see her under the best circumstances.'

'I hear she's remarried.'

'Yep. Good luck to her.'

'You know where she is?'

'Oh sure, but frankly she's of no interest to us. She'd have been incapable of doing him in, even if she'd wanted to, and anyway, she had a watertight alibi. In my view, she deserves to be left alone to get on with her new life.'

'I take it the second husband hadn't been waiting in the wings?'

Ferris gave a bark of laughter. 'You don't give up easily, do you? No, that I *did* check. They didn't even meet until Philpott had been dead a couple of years.'

'And he was an estate agent—Philpott, I mean: any dissatisfied customers? Anyone badly advised, overcharged, anything like that?'

'Nothing sufficiently serious for the firm to have heard about.'

'What firm was it?'

'Ward and Johnson, in Oxbury. Are you going to see them?'

Webb considered it, then shook his head. 'Not at this stage, Ted. I don't doubt your lads did a thorough job; the only reason I'm digging is in case there's a tie-in with the Judd inquiry. Talking of which, it's time I was getting back to it.'

'Not been much help, have I?' Ferris said ruefully, standing up with them.

'You've confirmed various points, which is

something. But now you've come back to it with a fresh mind, as it were, something might yet strike you. And if it does, needless to say, I'd like to hear about it.'

'Of course. And the same goes for me: if anything transpires in the new case which could be relevant to ours—'

'I'll be in touch double-quick, never fear.'

'Do you want to make a detour past the Feathers, Guv?' Jackson inquired as they got back into the car.

'Not much point, Ken, since Philpott wasn't known there.' He grinned. 'Or were you thinking it was getting on for lunchtime?'

Jackson's stomach was a useful timepiece, ensuring that at least they ate regularly.

'Well, now that you mention it—'

'I'd rather not waste any more time on Philpott just now. We'll set off for Ashmartin and stop somewhere on the way.'

'Right you are, Guv.'

Webb fastened his seat belt and, relieved as always to be leaving Erlesborough, settled down for the drive ahead.

CHAPTER THREE

'And he can't relax even now, because this TV interview's looming.'

Gillian turned back to the table with a

smile, to catch her friend absent-mindedly gazing out of the window.

'Sonia! I don't believe you've heard a word I've been saying!'

Sonia started guiltily. 'Sorry, I—'

Gillian looked at her more closely, then put the teapot on the table and sat down. 'Is something wrong?' she asked gently. 'You seem a bit—distracted.'

'It's probably nothing. I'll feel better after a cup of tea.'

Not wanting to press her, Gillian changed the subject. 'I don't often see you on a weekday. Have you been visiting a client?'

Sonia nodded. She was a private banking manager and spent much of her time calling on clients to assess their financial requirements. They'd been friends from schooldays, and in many ways Gillian felt closer to her than to her own sister. Sonia had been her bridesmaid, but she herself had married only three years ago, at the age of thirty-nine. While rejoicing for her, Gillian had not been entirely happy about her choice.

She passed a cup and saucer across the table. Then, sipping her own tea, she studied her friend. Sonia hadn't changed much since she was a leggy adolescent, though she'd acquired a certain grace. Her hair, centre-parted and hanging loosely about her face, was in the same style that she had worn at sixteen.

Now, however, it struck Gillian that the skin

was more tautly drawn over her cheekbones, there were shadows under her eyes and some fine little lines at their corners which she hadn't noticed before. Possibly—

Sonia said abruptly, 'I think Patrick is having an affair.'

Gillian, taken completely by surprise, could only stare at her, and she gave an uncertain laugh. 'How's that for a conversation stopper?'

'Tell me.'

'Oh, there's nothing definite.' Sonia's fingers were playing with her car keys. 'No more than a feeling, really. He just seems—different.'

'And that's all?'

She flushed. 'Except that when I hung up his jacket this morning, I thought I detected Chanel. I never wear it.'

'Oh, Sonia,' Gillian said softly.

'It's not only me who's noticed it; his mother and sister came for lunch on Sunday. I thought we were behaving perfectly normally, but when I went to get the coffee, Zoë followed me into the kitchen and asked if we'd had a row. You can imagine how I felt.

'And there's another thing,' she hurried on, before Gillian could comment. 'His mother's going downhill fairly rapidly, and I've a horrible feeling that when she dies, Patrick will expect Zoë to come and live with us.'

'Has he said so?'

'No, but you know how close they are. She

positively dotes on him, and he's so protective towards her. Damn it, she's over thirty, she should be able to fend for herself.' She added desolately, 'If she does come, it's I who'll be the odd one out.'

Gillian reached for her hand. 'I shouldn't worry about that, it might never happen. Tell me about Patrick—when did you begin to suspect?'

Sonia shrugged. 'It's been several months, I suppose, but it was only a vague feeling to start with, nothing I could tie down. Now—well, we don't seem to do much together any more. He's taken to going out by himself in the evening, to play golf or meet his friends for a drink. Or so he says,' she added in a low voice.

Gillian, watching her downcast face, felt a spurt of anger, and her thoughts went back to the first time she'd met Patrick Knowles, before he and Sonia were engaged. It had been at a Christmas party and, curious to meet the man who'd finally distracted Sonia from her career, she'd felt an instant disquiet. For had she met him under any other circumstances, she'd have written him off as one of life's bachelors, incapable of forming a lasting attachment to anyone. Which, as she'd told herself at the time, was grossly unfair on first acquaintance.

That he was a striking-looking man, she could not deny—over six feet tall, with a mane of pale hair already fading almost imperceptibly to grey. His eyes, also grey, were deep-set under jutting brows, which gave them a brooding quality, and he had a habit, which she found irritating, of constantly looking over the shoulder of the person to whom he was speaking, as though seeking a more interesting companion.

'Well, what do you think?' Sonia had demanded, the moment they were alone. 'Isn't he wonderful?'

'He's certainly attractive,' Gillian had hedged.

'I can't believe my luck, that he hasn't been snatched up long since!'

Looking at her glowing face, Gillian had not had the heart to voice her doubts. In any case, as she'd known even then, it would have made no difference. Sonia was head over heels in love, for probably the first time in her life, and no amount of logic would have persuaded her to think again. It gave Gillian no satisfaction that her initial instinct seemed to have proved correct.

'You could just be imagining it,' she suggested.

'I suppose so. But even if there's no one else, he doesn't seem interested in me.' She hesitated. 'I wonder if I could ask you a favour?'

'Of course.'

'Could you possibly invite us to dinner, and see what you think? If he strikes you as being any different?'

'If you feel it would help, of course I will.'

'I'd—like a second opinion,' Sonia said diffidently.

'Tell you what, I'll ask Alex and Roy as well—make it more of a party.'

'You won't say anything to them, will you?' Sonia asked anxiously.

'I wouldn't dream of it.' Gillian consulted the kitchen diary. 'We're booked up for the next few weekends; would midweek be OK?'

'Fine—we needn't stay late.'

'How about next Thursday, then—the first of August?'

Sonia bent to retrieve her handbag and fumbled in it for her diary. 'I've nothing on, but I can't speak for Patrick.'

'Well, let me know, and in the meantime I'll try Alex.'

Sonia stood up. 'Thanks, Gilly, I'm very grateful. I feel better already.' She looked round the familiar, sun-filled kitchen with its pretty wallpaper, its pine fittings, and the view of the canal from its window.

'I love this room,' she said. 'If it were my house, I'd spend most of my time in here! But I've kept you from your work long enough.' She bent forward and kissed Gillian's cheek. 'Bless you. I'll let you know if Patrick's free on Thursday.'

Gillian waited at the front door till she had reversed down the drive and, with a wave, disappeared from sight. Then, with a sigh, she went back to her studio.

*　　　*　　　*

The phone was ringing as Alex and the twins returned home, and she just managed to catch it before the answerphone cut in.

'Gilly, hi . . . Yes, I've just walked through the door. We've been to the parents for tea.'

Then, as her sister continued speaking, she tensed, gazing at her reflection in the hall mirror. Even when, minutes later, she replaced the phone, she continued to stare at her own face with its intent brown eyes and its frame of chestnut hair, as though she might find in it some solution to her dilemma.

Damn! she thought, moving at last and walking into the sitting-room. The twins had turned on the television and were sprawled on the floor watching it. Alex unlocked the patio door and went out on to the terrace, where she sat on the bench, hugging herself and gazing down the garden.

She'd been taken by surprise, rushing to answer the phone like that. Given time, she could have come up with some excuse—easy enough, in their busy lives. Now, it was too late. If she rang back and said Roy wasn't free next Thursday, she might be caught out in the lie. Come to that, Gilly might alter the date to accommodate them.

But God! she thought in panic, how can I spend an entire evening with Sonia and Patrick? Patrick. The name conjured him up and a wave of heat washed over her, leaving her weak. So far, they'd managed not to arouse suspicions, but in such a wide circle of friends she'd known they were playing with fire, that sooner or later—

She felt badly about Sonia, too, having known her most of her life. The trouble was that when she was with Patrick, all sense of what was right fled out of the window and she was left with only that deep and hungry need which was as new as it was basically unwelcome.

She'd been attracted to him from the start, at his and Sonia's engagement party, but only in a cursory way, as one sizes up the partners of one's friends. Since their wedding, she'd hardly seen them. Sonia was, after all, Gilly's friend rather than hers, and their paths seldom crossed.

Then, at the Country Club New Year party, when everyone was kissing everyone else, Patrick had suddenly said behind her, 'Happy New Year, Alex!' and pulled her against him. She closed her eyes on the memory, recalling the instant desire that had flared between them. Perhaps if she and Roy had not been having problems things might have been different, she might have drawn back, laughed it off. But in her uncertain and vulnerable

50

state, her willpower evaporated and she was lost.

She leant forward slowly and put her head in her hands, feeling the hot sun on the back of her neck. Next Thursday. A week tomorrow. It would be all right, she assured herself; no one suspected anything, no one would be watching them. All she had to do was behave naturally, and all would be well. It had to be.

*　　*　　*

Good's teams, Webb discovered, had been working diligently but without much success. On the plus side, house-to-house inquiries in Judd's own street had produced two witnesses who'd seen him set off for the fatal meeting. One man, watering his garden, had even had a word with him as he passed, but Judd had volunteered no information as to where he was going or whom he was meeting. They'd merely discussed the drought and the continuing heatwave.

His arrival at the rendezvous was, unfortunately, less well chronicled, though one of the Jester's clientele thought he remembered a man waiting on the corner as he went into the pub; his description was vague enough to fit Judd or a dozen other people.

Someone else, driving from the green, had had to swerve to avoid a car which stopped

51

suddenly outside the pub, but had not noticed the driver nor anyone on the pavement who might have been waiting to climb inside. The car was described as a dark-blue Honda with a fairly recent registration. This was now being sought on the PNC.

A couple of DCs had spent the previous evening at the Jester, asking questions and listening to the general conversation, to the resentment of the landlord, who accused them of putting off his customers. Several of them knew Judd, who occasionally had a bar lunch there, and all were adamant he'd not been in on Monday evening.

Finally, and not surprisingly, none of the offices in the same road as Social Services had anyone by the name of Mrs Fairlie working for them.

As a matter of routine, Webb had glanced through the list of Judd's most recent clients, though Steve Parker was convinced none of them was involved.

'You say he didn't recognize the voice,' Webb said, 'but suppose it was disguised?'

'It didn't strike him as being, just on edge.'

'On edge,' Webb repeated thoughtfully. He didn't press the point, but he still thought a client was the most likely bet. You heard of cases where normally sane people suddenly flipped, and after all, who else would have wanted to kill a man like Simon Judd?

And yet, he thought in exasperation, the

same question had applied to Trevor Philpott. Was it the same perpetrator in each case? They were uncannily alike—the decoy phone call, the pub meeting, the body left at another pub. Unless, of course, this latest was a copycat of the first one.

Before he left Ashmartin, news came through that the owner of the Honda had been traced. It belonged to a Mrs Castle, who admitted being in the vicinity of the green on Monday evening, and explained that she had braked suddenly to avoid a dog. She'd had a friend in the car with her, who verified her statement and confirmed that they had returned to the friend's house, where they'd spent the rest of the evening. They had seen no one waiting outside the Jester.

Not, as Webb remarked to Jackson on the way home, the most fruitful of days.

*   *   *

To his wife's frustration, Frederick was uncommunicative about his television interview, and became increasingly restless as the time for its transmission drew near.

'I'm not at all sure I shall bother watching it,' he announced. 'I know what I said, after all.'

'You most certainly will,' Edwina told him. 'I've no intention of sitting here all by myself. A little less of the false modesty, if you please.'

53

'It's not that,' he retorted. 'What irritated me is, we were supposed to be discussing *The Muddied Pool*, but I was inveigled into talking about the new book. You know how I hate doing that until it's all safely finished.'

'Think of it as advance publicity,' she advised serenely.

Even so, at nine o'clock it was necessary to call him in from the garden for the start of the programme. With a glance at the screen, he went to pour them both a glass of whisky before settling, with a resigned sigh, beside her.

Frederick now appeared on the screen, seated opposite Gregory Page, the programme's presenter.

'I'm glad we settled on that tie,' Edwina remarked with satisfaction. 'It looks most distinguished.'

'My dear, if you want to watch the programme, let us watch it, without a running commentary on my attire.'

She smiled and patted his hand, sensing his tension.

'Now, Mr Mace,' Page was saying, 'you're just back from a tour of Canada to promote your book, *The Muddied Pool*, which is described as—' he consulted the notes in front of him—'"an in-depth analysis of the criminal mind". Can you tell me—?'

The interview proceeded for several minutes along expected lines. It was, Edwina

54

thought, very similar to those she had sat through on the tour, and as a consequence Frederick was well versed in the answers and appeared relaxed and at his ease.

Then the camera turned to Page, who shifted in his chair as if preparing for a change of topic. 'I understand you've already made a start on your new book?'

Frederick's surprise was evident. 'Yes, I'm about halfway through.'

'Have you decided on the title?'

Frederick was silent for several seconds, looking down at his hands in his lap. Then, overcoming his reluctance to speak of it, he said, 'It will be called *The Ten Commandments.*'

Edwina, who hadn't known that, glanced at him, but he made no response.

'Dealing with the breaking of them, I presume?' the interviewer prompted.

'In a way, yes.'

Page gave a short laugh. 'Really, Mr Mace, you're being very reticent. Surely you can tell us something about it? I don't doubt your public out there are agog to know more.'

Frederick hesitated a moment longer, then appeared to admit defeat. 'Well, this might sound simplistic, but it struck me that if everyone kept the Ten Commandments, there would be virtually no crime.'

The camera panned in on Page's raised eyebrow, and Frederick went on quickly, 'Oh,

I'm aware that from the legal standpoint you can break all but three with impunity. Only murder, theft and false witness are criminal offences, but my point is that in a great many cases, the *motive* for a crime lies in someone *else*—possibly the victim himself—having broken a Commandment.'

'That's quite a contention.'

'But worth examining, I felt. So to illustrate the theory, I decided to study ten criminal cases, each of which could be linked with the breaking of a different Commandment, either in the crime itself or, of more interest to me personally, the motive behind it.'

He gave a slight smile. 'As you'll appreciate, it was necessary to go back quite a long way in respect of the first five, which, alas, only fundamental religions still adhere to. Taking the name of the Lord in vain is commonplace, we opted not to keep holy the Sabbath day, and so on. The flouting of those is unlikely to provoke any violent reaction today. However, by diligent searching—mainly on the part of my researcher, I hasten to add—we managed to find an example for each of them. I completed the chapter on number five just before leaving for Canada.'

That dry smile again. 'Lizzie Borden was, I felt, a prime, if somewhat extreme, illustration of not honouring her father and mother.'

Gregory Page leaned back in his chair. 'You've touched on some of the

56

Commandments, Mr Mace. Can you remind us—what are the rest of them?'

'The so-called "shalt nots". Murder is number six, and as well as being the ultimate crime, it frequently—to use the vernacular—*begets* murder. That is, it can lead to other, "revenge" killings—especially in the case of sectarian murders—thereby doubling as both crime and motive.

'Next we have adultery, no longer illegal in itself, but responsible for *crimes passionnels*—as also, of course, is number ten, not coveting your neighbour's wife.'

'Which we've all done at some time or another!' Page put in facetiously. 'Sorry—please go on.'

'*Thou shalt not steal,*' Frederick continued, 'is, as I mentioned, one of the three still indictable, and has a pretty broad scope—white-collar crime, fraud, unlawful possession. It, too, can be both motive and crime.

'Number nine, *Bearing false witness*, covers both perjury and, in today's parlance, "framing" someone, often causing grievances which result in violence; and the last part of the final Commandment, ordering us not to covet *anything* that belongs to someone else, embraces all the petty crimes which result from greed and envy.'

He lifted his hands. 'Have I proved my point?'

Page gave a laugh. 'I need notice of that

question, but you've certainly given us plenty to think about. Let's get down to specifics, then: this latest murder we have here in Broadshire: was a broken Commandment behind that?'

'My dear Mr Page, how could I know? I should have to study the case in detail before hazarding an opinion. No doubt the police have their theories, but I'm not privy to them.'

'The press are comparing it with another murder some years ago. Would you therefore expect the motives to be the same?'

'I admit I'm intrigued by the possibility; the more so, since I had the notion of including an unsolved crime among my ten, in the hope of discovering a new slant. By ironic chance, it was the murder of Trevor Philpott which I selected.'

Page leaned forward excitedly. 'How about that? And what was the motive for that one?'

'Oh, I've not started work on it yet. No, really—' He held his hands up as Page prepared to press him. 'I can't say any more about it at the moment.'

The interviewer, hiding his disappointment, leaned back again. 'Well, Mr Mace, it's been very interesting to talk to you, and I'm sure we've all learned something. I confess my knowledge of the Commandments was limited to the story of Moses coming down from Mount Sinai and saying to the Israelites, "Do you want the good news or the bad news?"'

He paused, as though expecting some reaction. Frederick merely waited.

'"The good news,"' Page continued, '"is that I kept Him down to ten. The bad news is that adultery's in."'

He laughed, and Frederick smiled politely. There was a final exchange of courtesies and the credits began to roll.

Edwina pressed the remote control and the screen went blank.

'Well, I must say you didn't *seem* reluctant to talk about it,' she remarked.

'That's just the trouble; once I let myself start, I say too much and then regret it.'

'I don't think you said too much,' she declared staunchly. 'I found it fascinating, and so, obviously, did Gregory Page. It will be interesting to read the reviews.'

Frederick said irritably, 'Did you notice he said "Si-ni-ai"? *Why* have people started doing that? For donkey's years we've learned about Moses bringing down the tablets from Mount Sinai—pronounced exactly as it's spelt—and now, for some unknown reason, everyone puts in the extra "i". No doubt some inexperienced newsreader started it, and everyone blindly followed suit. I even heard a clergyman say it, Lord help us.'

Edwina laughed and leaned over to kiss his cheek. 'I do love you,' she said.

*   *   *

59

'Well,' Hannah commented, switching off the set, 'what did you think of that?'

'Ve-ery interesting, as they used to say on the *Laugh-in*.'

'Seriously, though, do you think he has a point?'

'He might well have,' Webb conceded, 'though I don't see that it gets us much further.'

'Can *you* think of a crime that wasn't prompted by breaking one of the Commandments?'

'How about so-called mercy killing, allegedly done with the best of intentions?'

'"So-called", "allegedly"! You policemen! Anyway, some people don't regard that as a crime.'

'It is in the eyes of the law.'

'He came to talk to us at school once, Frederick Mace. He was excellent. Have you ever met him?'

'Not personally, though I've read his books. He gets carried away sometimes, like all these academics, but basically he's pretty sound.'

'It would be interesting to know if, when he's had time to study them, he concludes it was the same motive for both killings.'

'Whatever he concludes,' Webb responded, draining his glass, 'I sincerely hope we'll have beaten him to it. It's all very well for these writers; they can sit back and hum and haw for months on end. They haven't got the press or the Super on their backs wanting a quick result.'

'*Do* you think it's the same killer, David?'

'I hope so; it would be gratifying to clear up two cases at once.'

'That wasn't exactly what I asked.'

Webb smiled and got to his feet. 'Like your pal Mace, I can't say any more at the moment. In other words, I haven't a clue.'

It was, he reflected, as he went up the stairs to his own flat, a depressing admission on which to end the day.

CHAPTER FOUR

Paul Blake said over the phone, 'I enjoyed the interview, sir. Well done.'

Frederick smiled bleakly. 'Good of you, but I said more than I should, and now I've got the newshounds on my track. Serves me right, I suppose.'

'Yes, I've seen the papers. *"The answer to pub murders lies in the motives," says criminologist.* Are you still interested in meeting Philpott's widow?'

Frederick's hand tightened on the receiver. 'You've not tracked her down?'

'I have, as it happens. Following your instructions, I went to Oxbury yesterday and had lunch in the local pub. As you can imagine, this talk of links between the latest murder and Philpott's was the main topic of conversation. All well-trodden ground, of course, but then I really had a break. One of the men commented that the person he felt sorry for was Philpott's wife, having it all dragged up again.

'So I said casually, "She remarried, didn't she? What was the name again?"'

'And he said, "A chap called Bradburn. They moved down to Broadminster."'

'Well done, Paul. Do we know where in Broadminster?'

' We do. All I had to do was look them up in the phone book.'

Frederick said anxiously, 'She might not want to see me; she must have tried to put all that behind her.'

'Oh, I think she will, sir. Human nature being what it is.'

'How do you mean?'

'Well, you're not in the same category as the police or a common-or-garden reporter, are you? Even if she didn't watch the programme, she'll have seen today's papers. You're a celebrity, after all; she'll be flattered you want to see her. I suggest you give her a call.'

Frederick hesitated, his natural disinclination to intrude at war with his writer's curiosity. Then, well aware which would triumph, he said resignedly, 'Give me he number, then.'

*　　*　　*

A man's voice answered the phone, abrupt and impatient. It could be that Mrs Bradburn had already had more than enough calls that morning. However, on hearing Frederick's name, the tone changed.

'The one who was on the box last night?'

'I'm afraid so,' said Frederick deprecatingly.

'Just a minute.'

A woman's voice came on the line. 'Hello?'

'Mrs Bradburn? My name is Frederick Mace. I realize this is a difficult time and I'm sorry to trouble you. You might perhaps have heard that I'm studying your first husband's murder for my new book?'

'Did the same man kill the social worker?'

Straight to the point, which, thankfully, meant he needn't tread warily. 'It's possible, but I might have a clearer idea if we could discuss it personally, which is the reason for this call. May my assistant and I come to see you?'

A slight pause, while he held his breath. Then, 'I haven't anything new to add.'

'Even so, a first-hand account would help enormously.' He glanced at his watch, anxious to tie her down before she changed her mind. 'Would later this morning be convenient? We could be down in about an hour.'

63

He heard her sigh. Then she said, 'Very well. But I warn you, you might feel it's a wasted journey.' She cut short his protests. 'Have you got our address? It's off Lower Broad Street, just before you come to the hospital. Batchwood Drive, number twelve.'

'Thank you,' Frederick said, checking it against the address Paul had given him. 'I'm most grateful. In about an hour, then.'

*   *   *

On that sunny Saturday morning, the country road was clogged with caravans, joggers and cyclists. Frederick, checking his watch for the umpteenth time, said, 'What do we know about her? Anything?'

'Only that she and Philpott were married for ten years, very happily, it seemed. No children.'

Frederick lifted his briefcase and took out the notes he'd made while waiting for Paul to collect him, several sheets closely covered in his small, cramped handwriting.

'She sounded quite calm on the phone; I hope it won't upset her, resurrecting it all.'

'It's water under the bridge now, and she'll have her new husband for moral support.'

Something in his tone made Frederick glance at him sideways. Blake was a tall, thin young man with dry-looking dark hair and brown eyes which peered short-sightedly

64

hrough horn-rimmed spectacles. He was the deal researcher: thorough, efficient and meticulous. Frederick frequently marvelled at the speed with which he transcribed his own tightly packed pages into neat, easy-to-read print.

Of his private life, Frederick knew nothing, nor wanted to, grateful only that he had materialized in response to the advertisement for a researcher which he'd placed in a professional journal. He never spoke of family or friends or of his life before he came to Ashmartin, but there had been no cause to; theirs was, after all, a business relationship. All Frederick knew was that he was unmarried and had lodgings in Sheep Street, a location within five minutes' walk of the main library, which was doubtless why he'd chosen it.

'It's good of you to give up your Saturday morning,' he said suddenly, as the thought struck him for the first time.

Blake smiled. 'It's no hardship; I'm as interested as you are.'

They slowed down still further on the approach to Broadminster, entering the old town from the north east and filtering through the shoppers on to Broad Street before reaching Lower Broad Street and the turning to Batchwood Drive. The houses here were a mix of semidetacheds and bungalows, each in a colourful and well-kept garden. Paul pulled up outside number twelve, a bungalow, and both men got out into the stifling heat.

As they walked up the short path the front door opened and a tall, broad-shouldered man stood there. 'Peter Bradburn,' he said, holding out his hand. 'My wife's expecting you.'

She came forward as they were shown into the sitting-room, a small, pretty woman in her forties, wearing a print dress and sandals.

'We thought you might like coffee on the terrace? It's shaded out there at this time of day.'

'That's most kind of you.'

'Peter will take you through while I get the tray.'

'We sent the kids out to play, so we could have some peace,' Bradburn said, as they settled on the wrought-iron chairs.

'Oh? I understood—' Frederick began, before he could stop himself.

'My kids,' Bradburn explained, 'from my first marriage. We have them at weekends.'

'I see. Forgive me, it was just—'

'You're right, Aileen hasn't any of her own.'

'Did you know your wife's first husband, Mr Bradburn?'

'No,' Bradburn said, shaking his head for extra emphasis. 'I'd read about the murder, of course, but I didn't meet Aileen for a good two years after that—just, as luck would have it, as my own marriage was coming apart.'

'Has this latest case upset her?'

He shrugged. 'It's brought it back, naturally,

66

and all the speculation in the press hasn't helped.'

'I'm afraid I added to that,' Frederick admitted ruefully.

'Well, as I said to Aileen, once you've featured in a murder case, you're considered public property.'

'Not by me, I assure you. If you'd rather I didn't—'

'Is Pete being overprotective?' Aileen Bradburn asked, setting down a tray with coffee cups and a plate of biscuits. She flashed her husband a smile. 'It's all right, love. I wouldn't have agreed to see them if I hadn't felt up to it.'

Frederick, still diffident about questioning her, was reassured.

She handed him a cup and saucer. 'Anyway, Mr Mace, I was interested in your ideas on motives.'

'You saw the programme?'

'Oh, yes, I watch everything to do with crime.'

She glanced at him, catching his surprise, and smiled. 'Perhaps I should explain; when Trevor—died, I buried my head in the sand, and for years I mentally blocked out any news items about murder or death of any kind. But later, when it started to fade a bit, I suppose I went to the other extreme. I think I reasoned that if I watched and read everything I could about it, I might somehow work out why it

67

happened.

'Do you see what I mean? It would have been different if the killer had been caught; then I'd have been able to face it, come to terms as you have to with any death. But I was still living in Oxbury then, and I used to find myself looking at people I passed in the street, thinking, "It could have been him."'

'That's very understandable.'

She nodded, satisfied, and settled back, sipping her coffee. 'So—what is it you want to ask me?'

'Before I start, would you mind if we switched on a recorder? It makes life so much simpler these days.'

'I've no objection.'

Frederick nodded to Blake, who took one out of his pocket and laid it on the table alongside the tray.

'I realize, Mrs Bradburn, that you gave a detailed statement to the police at the time, but that was strictly facts, and I'd like to try a different approach. You've now had time to look back—and I'm sure you've done so many times—over the weeks and months leading to your husband's death. That is what I'd like you to speak about—his character, his friends, his attitudes, your own relationship with him, and whether it changed immediately before his murder. In fact, anything unusual that might have taken place. But first, have you by any chance a photograph? The ones I've seen in the papers aren't too clear.'

'Yes, I—still have some old albums somewhere.'

'I'll get them,' Bradburn said, getting to his feet and going in through the patio door.

'How will seeing his photograph help?' Aileen asked curiously.

Frederick smiled. 'After motives, my main interest is faces; I believe they give away far more of our character than we realize. Oh, I know the old chestnut about murderers looking like the boy next door, and they might well do so. But if you study—really study—their features, there are often clues to be found.'

'But Trevor wasn't a murderer,' Aileen protested.

'It goes for all of us. Little traits in our characters leave traces which can be read if one knows what to look for.'

She moved uncomfortably. 'It hardly seems fair, searching for faults in the victim.'

'I didn't specify faults,' Frederick reminded her. 'Good traits are also to be found. But whichever, surely it's acceptable to look for them if they point to the motive for murder?'

She lifted her eyebrows. 'Back to the Ten Commandments?'

'In all probability the breaking of one.'

Bradburn returned with an album, still in its Cellophane cover. 'I presume it's the latest one you want?'

'Thank you, yes.'

Frederick took it from him, resting it on his knees while he extracted his glasses from his pocket and put them on. The album was dated six years previously, and he began slowly turning the pages until he came to a clear photograph of Philpott. He was seated at a cafe table—somewhere in Europe, by the look of it—and staring straight at the camera.

Frederick sat for several minutes letting his eyes move slowly over the face in front of him. If he knew nothing of this man, what would his appearance have told him? That he was confident, perhaps a trifle arrogant, judging by the tilt of his head. And, even more clearly than in the blurred newspaper print, he was again conscious of his likeness to Roger Denby, the man he'd known years before who had a reputation as a philanderer. An expression in the eyes, the set of the mouth— Was it fair, on that basis, to tar Philpott with the same brush?

He looked up, meeting Aileen's gaze. 'I presume the marriage was happy, Mrs Bradburn?' That was the story that emerged at the time.

Was there, perhaps, just the slightest hesitation before she nodded? He couldn't be sure.

'There's nothing you'd like to add? You realize, I hope, that this isn't idle curiosity?'

For a moment longer she sat staring into

70

her coffee cup. Then, with a glance at her husband, she said flatly, 'I wasn't lying, Mr Mace; as far as I was concerned, our marriage *had* been happy, and I told the police so at the time. Oh, we had the odd tiff, and I suppose, looking back, it wasn't all rosy, but it never occurred to me there was anything wrong.'

'Until —?' he prompted gently.

'Yes, you're right—until last year, when I met a couple Trev and I'd been friendly with. We used to see quite a lot of them, till they moved away and we lost touch.

'Then last summer, we met quite by chance—at the races, of all places; Pete had taken me to the Broadminster Cup. Well, he and Jerry went off to place some bets, and Debs said something about what a nice chap Pete seemed. Then she added, "Much more your type than Trevor. I often wondered how you put up with him."

'She must have seen my face, because she suddenly went scarlet and said, "Me and my big mouth!" I asked her what she meant and she didn't want to say, but I finally wheedled it out of her. Apparently, one evening at the cricket club, Trevor'd had too much to drink, and Jerry walked him home. On the way, Trev had suddenly started bragging about various women he was seeing, and offered to fix Jerry up, if he was interested.'

Frederick could not resist a glance of triumph at Paul. The memory of Roger Denby had not, after all, let him down.

'The next morning he rang to apologize,' Aileen was continuing. 'He was terribly embarrassed, Debs said, tried to make out he'd been pulling Jerry's leg, and asked him to forget it.'

Frederick said sympathetically, 'It must have been a tremendous shock.'

'Yes; I couldn't help wondering whether he'd have gone on having girlfriends for the rest of his life, and then I started remembering all kinds of little things—the times he'd cancelled something we were doing because he "couldn't get away", evenings when he was supposed to be showing people round houses, things like that.

'Of course,' she finished wretchedly, 'it might all have been quite genuine, but once the doubts were there, they tarnished everything.'

'Have you any idea when that incident took place? How near to your husband's death?'

'She didn't say; but they left Oxbury about a year before it happened, so at least that long.'

'Do you know if he actually named these women?'

'I've no idea. Debs certainly didn't.'

Even if he had, Frederick thought, 'Jerry' would be unlikely to remember after all this time—unless, of course, he'd known those concerned. But in any case, Philpott had probably met the crucial one during the last year of his life; it was doubtful if his affairs would have lasted longer than a few months. All the same—

'Have you mentioned this to the police?' he asked.

It was Bradburn who answered. 'There didn't seem much point. It was all pretty vague, and we couldn't see what help it would be after all this time.'

'It might at least provide a motive.' Frederick turned back to Aileen. 'The police do know where you are?'

'Yes, but I'm of no interest to them; I told them all I knew.' She met his eye. 'Well, I did at the time. Ought I to contact them, do you think?'

'It would do no harm.'

'You think the same man might have done it, then?' It was the second time she'd asked that question, but Frederick was still not ready to answer it. Instead, he countered it with one of his own.

'Can you think of anything else your husband did that might have caused trouble or resentment? Had he, for instance, any particular prejudices—racial, perhaps, or even sexual?'

She started to shake her head, then paused, frowning a little. Frederick leant forward.

'You've remembered something?'

'Well, not really. I mean, it wasn't anything much—in fact, I'd forgotten all about it.

Talking of Debs and Jerry must have brought it back.'

'Go on, Mrs Bradburn.'

She gave a dismissive little gesture. 'Really, it's nothing. Not even worth mentioning.'

'Please.'

'Well, it was one evening at the cricket club. We were sitting on the verandah after some match or other, and Trev and Jerry went inside for more drinks. When they came back, Trev was flushed and muttering something about "bloody perverts", and Jerry said he'd had to drag him away because he'd insulted some gay men at the bar. And that was it, really.' She paused. 'Sorry, but when you mentioned prejudices, it just reminded me.'

'Was your husband openly hostile to homosexuals?'

'Oh no, not at all. I think it was just that he'd been drinking, and he made some off-the-cuff comment which they reacted to.'

'Nothing like that ever happened again?'

She shook her head decidedly. 'Never.'

'And you never heard him make any racial comments which could have caused offence?'

She looked distressed and Peter Bradburn, frowning, moved to her side.

'No, definitely not. I feel awful, now, having told you—it gives quite the wrong impression of Trev. All right, he was a bit of a Jack-the-lad—more than I realized at the time—but there was nothing vindictive about him.

74

Basically, he was—a nice man.'

She sounded close to tears, and as her husband bent to comfort her, Frederick nodded to Paul to switch off the recorder.

'I'm sorry, Mrs Bradburn, I didn't mean to upset you. Please forgive me.'

'I'm just sorry I mentioned it, that's all.'

'I shouldn't let it worry you. We all say things we don't mean, at some time or other.'

'Yes.' She brightened. 'I'm sure that's all it was.'

He rose to his feet. 'We've taken up quite enough of your time. I'm extremely grateful to you for being so frank with me.'

As they walked together back through the house, Bradburn remarked, 'You never made any comment on the photograph, Mr Mace. Was it any help?'

'Yes, indeed; that's why I asked Mrs Bradburn about her marriage.'

Bradburn turned to stare at him. 'You're telling me you could tell from Trevor's photo that he was unfaithful?'

'I got an impression, that's all. I assure you, Mr Bradburn, there's no magic involved. There are people who make a profession out of such studies, and they've solved some pretty complex cases on the basis of them.'

'Nice woman,' he commented to Paul as they got into the car. 'But for all her defence of him, I don't think I should have cared much for Trevor Philpott. And I was right, wasn't I, about the womanizing. If you can find me a photograph of Judd, we'll see if we have the same luck there. First, though, I'd like to visit the firm where Philpott worked—what was it called?'

'Ward and Johnson.'

'That's right. It'll be interesting to know if anyone there knew of his peccadilloes.'

'But you don't want to go there now, surely? It's a hell of a round trip—a good hour from here to Oxbury, and the best part of two from there back to Ashmartin. Won't your wife be expecting you?'

'I didn't put a time on it, but I'll phone and let her know what we're doing. In the meantime, we'll have some lunch before we set off. There's a pleasant place in Monk's Walk, I remember.'

*   *   *

The cathedral and metropolitical church of St Benedict in Broadminster, commonly known as Broad Minster, lay at the heart of the town, a glorious Gothic extravaganza soaring upwards into the summer sky. Having of necessity parked their car some distance from the centre, they came upon it suddenly as they turned into Monk's Walk which fringed the green in front of it, and as always Frederick felt his heart lift.

'A wonderful sight, isn't it?' he said,

76

stopping abruptly on the pavement the better to gaze, and causing some muttering among the people directly behind him. 'I used to sing in the choir there as a boy.'

'The sight on the green isn't quite so inspiring,' Paul commented drily, nodding across the road. On this Saturday lunchtime the grass was covered with families enjoying picnics, children playing, and sunbathers, their clothes inelegantly bunched up or pushed down, making the most of the sunshine.

Frederick laughed. 'Good luck to them. Now, if I remember correctly there's an excellent wine bar along here which will do us nicely.'

As they sat over poached salmon and salad, Paul said curiously, 'Do you think this story of Philpott's playing around really has a bearing on his death?'

Frederick refilled his glass. 'All I know is that a motive was never discovered, and we might now have unearthed one. Or even two, come to that; the homosexual angle might bear looking into.'

'Surely not; from the sound of it, it was only a drunken insult.'

'*In vino veritas*. If he really considered them "bloody perverts", it might have come out again, with more serious consequences. Still, I tend to agree with you; I think it's the women who will prove to be more pertinent.'

'What about Judd?' Blake asked after a

moment. 'Are you hoping to suss a motive from *his* photograph?'

'Possibly,' Frederick replied imperturbably, 'but that's not all we have to go on. You're forgetting that in each case the most conclusive evidence could be the voice of the murderer on the telephone. And voices, like faces, give away more than their owners realize.'

He reached for his wallet and extracted a newspaper clipping from it. 'I cut this out of the *News* the other evening.' He unfolded it, fumbled on his glasses, and read aloud: '*Diane Pearcy, 32, the receptionist at the Department who took the call, described the speaker as sounding nervous. Pressed further, she stated that the voice was male, light in tone, with a local accent. He asked for Mr Judd by name, and she assumed he was a client.*'

'If you're hoping to compare that with Philpott's killer,' Paul said, 'there was no description of his voice in any of the papers I went through.'

Frederick refolded the clipping, put it back in his wallet, and removed his glasses. 'I know,' he said, picking up his knife and fork again. 'I went through them, too. But with luck, whoever received the call might still work at the firm.'

'The police will have checked it out, surely.'

'I don't doubt it, my boy, but they're unlikely to pass any information on to me. I'm

78

not working for the police, I'm working for myself and my book.'

To which Paul could find no reply.

*   *   *

The town of Oxbury was noted firstly for its boys' public school, Greystones College, and secondly for being built on the Kittle, one of Broadshire's most attractive rivers.

Again they had trouble parking, and again people were out in their hundreds along the river banks. Having circled a multistorey twice, they were fortunate enough to have a motorist pull out just in front of them, and slid into the space ahead of another driver approaching from the opposite side.

'An omen, perhaps,' Frederick said as they got out. 'Let's hope our luck holds.'

The offices of Ward and Johnson on the High Street were fronted by large plate-glass windows, through which they could see a row of desks, each with someone behind it and a couple of people seated opposite.

'The property market seems to be booming,' Frederick commented, 'which is not what one reads in the papers.'

Though he had phoned his wife from the wine bar, he'd ignored Paul's suggestion of booking an appointment with Ward and Johnson, and Paul, following him inside, wondered if the estate agents would be too busy this Saturday afternoon to deal with an elderly gentleman and his questions on what happened here six years ago.

They stood inside the door for several minutes without attracting so much as a glance. No doubt it was assumed they were awaiting a vacant desk. Then Frederick's patience gave out. 'See what you can do, Paul,' he said testily, shifting his weight. 'There's a door down at the bottom there—probably the manager. Flush him out, there's a good chap.'

Expecting a rebuff, Paul did as he was asked, and was relieved to discover that once again Frederick's television interview stood in his stead.

'I was about to send you packing,' the manager admitted. 'We've had the police and the press sniffing round again this week and quite frankly we had enough of that at the time. However, if Mr Mace would like a word, of course I'll be glad to help if I can.'

Paul turned and beckoned Frederick, who hurried to join him, seating himself gratefully on the chair indicated.

'This is kind of you, Mr Laycock,' he began, having noted the name on the door as he came in. 'I have a couple of questions, if you can spare the time. The first is a delicate one: could you tell me whether there were any rumours about Mr Philpott's—er—having an eye for the ladies?'

The manager shook his head. 'No, the

police asked that at the time. There wasn't so much as a hint of gossip—and he'd a very pleasant wife.'

'His name was never even casually linked with anyone else?'

'Not in my hearing, and I'm sure that goes for the rest of the firm. Of course, several of those who knew him have moved on now; in fact, come to think of it, most of our present personnel have joined us since his death.'

'Not whoever took the phone call that day?' Frederick demanded urgently. 'That person's still here?'

Laycock frowned. 'I'm not sure it wasn't Trevor himself.'

Frederick stared at him in consternation. Was that why there'd been no description of the voice among the papers? But as this setback stared him in the face, Laycock went on, 'No—wait a minute—I remember now. It was Sandra, I'm sure it was. Would you like to speak to her?'

Frederick, weak with relief, could only nod. Laycock picked up the phone. 'Sandra, when you've finished what you're doing, would you come in, please?'

She proved to be a freckle-faced young woman with curly hair, who looked a little harassed. It was hot in the outer office with all that glass, and her nose was shining. However, though she hadn't seen Frederick's programme, she'd read about it, and was obviously overcome to be speaking to someone she regarded as famous.

'Yes,' she replied when the question was put to her, 'I took the call. He sounded nice—like a gentleman. I couldn't believe, afterwards, that it was him.'

'By "like a gentleman",' Frederick asked her, 'do you mean he hadn't a Broadshire accent?'

'Oh no, sir, he was very well spoken. Polite, too.'

'Did he sound nervous in any way?'

'Not at all, cool as you please. He said, "Would it be possible to have a word with Mr Philpott?"'

'Was his voice deep or light?'

She thought back. 'Medium, I'd say. He sounded nice. Just shows you, doesn't it?'

'When you handed the phone to Mr Philpott, what did he say?'

She flushed. 'I didn't listen, sir. A couple had sat down at my desk and I went over to attend to them. The police asked me the same thing, whether Trevor made any note of the man's name or anything, but all he wrote on the pad was: *The Stag—nine pm.*'

'The Stag?' Frederick repeated. 'Not the Feathers?'

'No, sir, the Stag, here in town. He must have arranged to meet the man there and then been—been taken to the Feathers later.' She bit her lip.

Just as Judd had met someone at the Jester and been taken to the Nutmeg. Yet another similarity. So far, only the voice seemed different.

Once again, Frederick courteously thanked his informants for their time and, deep in thought, returned with Paul to their car and settled down for the long drive back to Ashmartin.

CHAPTER FIVE

That same afternoon, Webb received a phone call from DCI Good.

'Spot of good news, Dave: bloke by the name of Bragg rang in. He's been abroad for a couple of days and has just read all the hoo-ha in the press. Thinks he might have seen our lad arriving at the Nutmeg.'

'Go on.'

'Says he was leaving the pub and about to turn left towards Ashmartin when he saw this car approaching at speed with its indicator flashing, and it swerved into the "In" gateway. The chap in the passenger seat was lolling all over the place, only kept in place by his seat belt, by the look of it. Bragg remembers thinking he'd already had more than enough.'

'Did he get a look at the driver?'

'No, the passenger was on his side, and

83

anyway it was all over in seconds.'

'What time was this?'

'About nine-fifteen, he reckons.'

'And from his description, Judd was already dead?'

'I'd say so, or close to it.'

'What about the car?'

'More help on that one: light-coloured Ford Escort, three or four years old, sun visor, faulty near-side brake light.'

'Too much to hope for the reg. ?'

There was a smile in Good's voice. 'Have a heart, Dave. So, we've started another round of inquiries in the town centre and at local garages. Someone might recognize the description.'

'Ten to one it'll turn out to be stolen.'

'Even so, there could be bloodstains on the passenger seat.'

'Well, let's hope the PNC comes up with something. Thanks, Harry.' Webb dropped the phone on its cradle, pushed back his chair and went into the outer office.

'Come on, Ken, we're off to Ashmartin again.'

In the car on the way there, Webb told him the latest development. 'I want another word with Mrs Judd,' he finished. 'She should be over the initial shock, and might have remembered something relevant.'

Jackson slowed the car to allow a couple with a toddler to cross the road. Webb said,

'Sorry to keep you from the family on a Saturday, Ken.'

'That's all right, Guv. In any case, Millie's taken the kids to her mother's for the weekend.'

'You should have gone with them?'

'I'll survive. Had Judd any kids?'

'Two, I believe, five and seven.'

They drove in silence into the town, took a left-hand turn before reaching the green, and followed the road uphill past the Queen Elizabeth Hospital to Chestnut Drive, where the Judds lived. The children Webb had just mentioned were playing in the front garden, chasing each other and laughing. Thank God kids were so resilient, he thought as he pushed open the gate.

His ring was answered by a woman in her fifties. Webb introduced himself and Jackson, and she nodded.

'I'm Ella's mother. You'd better come in.'

Ella Judd came into the hall to meet them, drying her hands on her apron.

'Sorry to trouble you,' Webb said, 'but we've a few more questions, I'm afraid.'

She led the way into the front room and her mother, after hesitating a moment, went back to the kitchen.

'Mrs Judd, I'd like you to tell me everything you can about your husband's friends and colleagues. Was there anyone he was particularly close to? At the office, for instance?'

She pressed her hands together. 'He got on well with all of them, but I wouldn't say he was *close*. He didn't see them out of office hours.'

'Who did he know socially, then?'

'Well, there's Bill Price, I suppose, but really Simon was a home bird. He met so many people during working hours, often in very distressing circumstances, that when he came home, he just wanted to relax with me and the children.'

Price's name and phone number were noted. It didn't seem much to go on.

'Can you remember anyone else he might have mentioned?' Webb persisted. 'Someone who'd been in some sort of trouble, perhaps?'

She smiled sadly. 'Most of his clients were in trouble, Mr Webb. That's why they went to him, but he never talked to me about them.'

'What about the man he was meeting on Monday?'

'Jim Fairlie.' She said the name thoughtfully.

'He did mention him, then?'

'Yes; when he came in, he asked me if I remembered him speaking of anyone by that name.'

'And did you?'

'No. He told me this man had rung him and said they'd met on some course, but he didn't remember, and various other names the man reeled off didn't ring a bell, either. But Simon was always bad on names—we used to tease him about it.' Her eyes filled with tears.

It tied in with what Steve Parker had told them. Webb had hoped Judd might have said more to his wife, but it seemed not.

'But you gathered it was a professional rather than a social call?'

'I suppose so, since he had a problem to discuss.'

Webb thought for a moment. He'd more or less dismissed the claimed acquaintanceship as a ploy to coerce Judd into a meeting—but suppose it was true? Could Judd have injured someone seriously enough to warrant his own death, when he couldn't even remember meeting the man?

'Did he get any personal calls at work?'

'You'd have to ask the Department. I only phoned there if it was urgent.'

'And you can't remember having heard of Jim Fairlie before? Not just recently, but in the past?'

'No—and I've a good memory, Simon used to rely on me. But it wouldn't have been his real name, would it? You'd hardly give that over the phone, when you were planning to—to—' She came to a halt, and after a moment added unsteadily, 'If he had done, I might have recognized it.'

'Thank you, Mrs Judd,' Webb said gently. 'Now, if you don't mind we'd like to take a look at your husband's papers—letters, insurance policies, his will, anything personal he kept at home.'

'I doubt if it'll help.' Ella Judd went over to the desk against the wall. 'Simon went through his papers regularly, throwing away everything that had been dealt with. He never kept letters once they'd been answered.'

Webb could have wished he'd been less methodical.

She watched while they systematically worked through the folders. As she'd intimated, the paperwork was minimal and everything neatly in place. As with Judd's office files, there was nothing at all to give them a lead to his death.

Resignedly, Jackson stacked the papers and replaced them in the various drawers. Another necessary task completed, Webb reflected as he watched him, and, like many another, it had got them precisely nowhere.

*   *   *

It was the normal practice for the family to gather for lunch at Brighton Villa on the first Sunday of the month. However, since she and Frederick had been away at the beginning of July, Edwina had decided this month to bring the arrangement forward a week. It seemed a long time since they'd all been together and she was looking forward to seeing them, albeit with underlying anxiety. Alex had been

88

singularly uncommunicative when she and the boys came for tea; by actually seeing her with Roy and watching the interaction between them, it should be easier to gauge how things were.

Not, she told herself hotly, as this thought occurred to her, that she was spying on them; she merely wanted to satisfy herself that things had not deteriorated during her absence.

She came out of the kitchen and paused in the hallway, enjoying the sunlight which streamed through the pane in the front door and burnished the polished floor. No fitted carpets at the villa, just the lovely old boards and a selection of pretty, if faded, rugs.

She particularly loved the house on these family days, when it really came alive. It was a house meant to echo with running footsteps, voices calling, laughter. She supposed it was too big for their present needs, but could imagine living nowhere else. No modern flat could hold all their treasures, amassed over a long and happy lifetime, let alone their large furniture, which varied from valuable antiques to shabby but equally loved pieces bought at the salerooms in the early days of their marriage. And Frederick, she thought fondly, would wilt if his desk was moved from the window overlooking the green.

She frowned suddenly, remembering her husband's account of his previous day's sleuthing. It was all very well to concern

89

himself with crimes which had been neatly rounded off and their perpetrators either locked away or dead. She was not so happy with his probing a live one, as it were, one which, following through the metaphor, might go off in his face.

She gave a little shiver, then told herself she was being fanciful. If the entire Broadshire police force had not tracked down the murderer over the last six years, it was unlikely in the extreme that Frederick would stumble over him.

Except, added that inner voice worriedly, that the case had been resurrected with this new murder. Even if two different killers were involved, it was a reminder that the first one was still around.

*　　*　　*

The lunch went well. Alex chatted and laughed, Roy was almost defiantly relaxed, Gilly and Hugh were their usual dear, dependable selves. Loveday looked uncannily as Gilly had at her age, Edwina thought; the same clear blue eyes and that silver-blonde hair hanging down her back. They had both inherited Frederick's colouring, Alex and the boys hers. Looking round the table, she felt an almost unbearable love for them all. Please keep them safe, she prayed spontaneously, then instantly mocked herself. What was the

matter with her today? The next thing, she'd
be reading tea-leaves.

'If you children have finished, you may leave
the table,' she said, as she always did before
the coffee was served.

'Thanks, Gran.' Toby and Jack slid off their
chairs and disappeared in the direction of the
garden. Edwina turned to her granddaughter.
'You're also excused, dear, if you'd like to go.'

Loveday, who jealously maintained her four
years' seniority over the twins, flashed her a
smile. Caught in the in-between stage and
bored equally by her young cousins and the
conversation of her elders, she was grateful for
her grandmother's understanding.

'I did bring a book with me,' she admitted.

'The lounger's under the apple tree.'

'Brilliant!' And she, too, was gone. On cue,
Mrs Davidson, who had been with the Maces
for the last twenty years, brought in the coffee
cups.

'I hope you're all coming to Frederick's talk
on Tuesday,' Edwina said, pouring the strong,
dark liquid. 'It's at the Central Library, eight
o'clock.'

'Good gracious me,' Frederick protested,
'it's not a command performance! There's no
compulsion about it.'

Gillian laughed and laid a hand on his arm.
'Of course we're coming, Pop! Try keeping us
away. What's the title of it?'

'"Murder Under the Microscope". It's a

dissertation, really, on the way I examine crime.'

'With questions from the floor afterwards?'

He grimaced. 'Unfortunately, yes. I usually enjoy that part, but they're sure to ask about the pub murders. It's my own fault, for allowing myself to be drawn on television. I should have known better.'

'But what's wrong with discussing them?' Alex asked.

'Well, I'm studying the first for my new book, and as you know, I dislike talking about current work. As for the second, I don't know any more about it than anyone else. Anyway, the police might take a dim view of my holding forth.'

'I don't see why; it's no different, surely, from all the speculation in the press?'

'No, I suppose it isn't. I mustn't give myself delusions of grandeur.'

'You'll have to put plants in the audience, Frederick,' Hugh said humorously, 'to ask the questions you're prepared to answer.'

'Well, I'll be there rooting for you,' Alex declared, 'though I can't speak for Roy. He has his own priorities these days.'

Edwina's stomach lurched. From the corner of her eye she saw Roy's hand clench on the table, but he said levelly, 'I certainly hope to be; it should be a most interesting evening.'

'More interesting than your sons' Sports Day?'

Roy raised his hand and brought it sharply down on the table, making the spoon dance in his saucer. 'I thought you'd find a way to bring that up.'

Frantically, Edwina lifted the coffee pot. 'Anyone ready for a refill?'

No one answered; the atmosphere had suddenly become charged. Alex turned to her, her voice vibrating with tension.

'You know how the boys look forward to Sports Day—specially this year, when, as I told you in my letter, both of them were picked for their house teams. They even persuaded Roy to volunteer for the Fathers' Race. *Then* what do you think happens? The day before, there's a hitch at some office in Glasgow, and off he flies without a backward glance. *Glasgow!* You'd have thought they could have found someone nearer, wouldn't you?'

Roy said tightly, 'Alex is convinced I arranged it all deliberately, even though I explained it was my programme that had gone wrong, and I was responsible for it. I still hoped to be back in time, but the sorting out took longer than expected.'

'But it was the *weekend*, Roy. It could have waited till Monday, specially when you'd something important on.'

'Even if it was Christmas, it would have made no difference. If I hadn't seen to it at once, they'd have lost millions of pounds' worth of orders. But you wouldn't see that.

You took it as a personal slight—as, let's face it, you take most things these days.'

'It was because of the boys,' she said shakily. 'They won their races, and you weren't there to see them. Toby was in tears afterwards.' She sounded close to them herself.

Frederick cleared his throat. 'Well, it was disappointing, of course, but it's not the end of the world, now, is it? I'm sure Roy—'

Alex pushed back her chair and stood up. 'If that's all the support I'm getting, I'll spare you any further embarrassment and take Goldie for a walk.' The long-haired retriever, asleep by Frederick's chair, thumped his tail at the sound of his name.

'Come along, boy! Walk!' she repeated sharply. The dog sat up, surprised at the break in his routine, then, as she patted her thigh, got to his feet and trotted after her out of the room.

There was an awkward silence. Then Roy said flatly, 'I'm sorry. I shouldn't have risen to that. We've spoiled your lunch party.'

He looked round at their grave faces. 'I'm sure you all know we've been having problems. I just don't know how to handle it. I still love her, but she won't let me near her. Everything I do seems to irritate her.'

'She's very unhappy,' Edwina said quietly.

'She's not the only one, but she absolutely refuses to discuss it. Do you think one of you could have a word with her?'

94

'I have tried, Roy,' Gillian said, 'but I didn't get very far, either.'

'I think, my dear,' Frederick remarked, 'you'd better try again. Things can't be allowed to go on like this, for the boys' sakes as much as anyone's. And talking of the boys, it's time we went outside to join them.'

Gillian met Roy's anxious eyes. 'All right,' she told him, 'I'll have another go.' And, already regretting the promise she'd been forced into, she followed her mother out to the garden.

*　　　*　　　*

It was a day for family meals, but Sonia, whose working week tended to be fraught, found herself resenting the unspoken assumption that each Sunday, month in, month out, Patrick's mother and sister would come to lunch.

It would be pleasant, she thought, making the mint sauce, to have a Sunday alone together. They could laze in the garden, perhaps go for a pub lunch, recoup their forces for the following week.

As it was, preparations for the meal spilled over into Saturday, dominating the whole weekend. Unless she'd managed to shop after work, it meant trailing out to the supermarket, where she'd stare hopelessly at the shelves seeking inspiration. All of which took time she could ill afford, since Saturday was also the day on which the household chores must be done; the house had to be cleaned, the washing seen to, and everything tidied away for the Sunday visitors.

It seemed they had no time alone, and with her fears about Patrick's straying attention, she was even more conscious how much they needed it.

His voice broke into her thoughts. 'They're here!'

She heard him walk through the hall, open the front door and go out on to the gravel to meet them. Sighing, she took off her apron, and went to join him.

As they sat over their pre-lunch sherries, Sonia surreptitiously studied her in-laws. Sybil Knowles must have been pretty at one time, but years of suffering from a debilitating illness had taken their toll. Though she'd never been anything other than pleasant, Sonia felt Sybil resented her, would have preferred Patrick's attention to have remained fixed solely on herself and her daughter.

And Zoë seemed to be a replica of her mother. In her case, the prettiness had not quite gone, lingering in the grey eyes and thick fair hair she shared with her brother. But she was pale while Patrick was tanned, small where he was tall, timid while he was outgoing, and altogether seemed much younger than she actually was.

She had had a breakdown some years previously and her mother and brother continued to treat her as an invalid. However, it seemed to Sonia that she played on her fragility, and was actually capable of doing more than she admitted. The fear which she'd voiced to Gillian, that on Mrs Knowles's death Zoë would move in with them, returned, filling her with dread.

'We thought we might go away for a few days,' Zoë was saying, 'just for a little break, to give Mother a change of scene.'

'Good idea,' Patrick said heartily, refilling Sonia's glass. (Sybil and Zoë had both refused a top-up, making her feel like a seasoned toper.) 'Where will you go?'

'Oh, not far. Up into the Cotswolds, probably. As you know, I'm not a very confident driver.'

'If you want to go farther afield, I could always run you there,' Patrick volunteered. 'And collect you, when you're ready to come home.'

'Oh, we couldn't expect you to do that!' Zoë protested, but Sonia knew, from her satisfied expression, that it was, in fact, exactly what she'd expected.

'Nonsense. Just say the word.'

'Well, we had talked about the Lake District—' Zoë's voice tailed off.

Sonia heard herself say, 'There are always trains, you know, if you don't want to drive.'

They all turned to look at her, three Knowles faces expressing surprise. For an uncomfortable moment, she felt a complete outsider. Then Sybil said equably, 'Of course there are. Sonia wants Patrick to spend his weekends with her, dear, not ferrying us around the country. It's only natural.'

'In that case,' Zoë said with a small sigh, 'we'll stick with the Cotswolds. You know you couldn't cope with a long train journey.'

Sonia wanted to protest that a train was more comfortable, allowed more room, provided meals, but she'd already said too much and had been subtly wrong-footed for doing so. Instead, she smiled brightly. 'I'll go and make the gravy,' she said.

Out in the kitchen, though, she felt ashamed of herself. Between them, they'd made her look selfish and ungracious—and perhaps she was. It had, after all, been kind of Patrick to offer his help; she knew he felt responsible for them, and their claim on him predated her own. He'd been taking care of them since he was fifteen, when his father died. Her intervention had been petty and, she admitted, motivated by jealousy.

Resolving from now on to brim over with charity, Sonia took the joint out of the oven.

*   *   *

The studio was flooded with the mellow

evening light. Hugh stood in the doorway with two glasses of wine and looked across at his wife, who was staring out of the window.

'I thought you were working. I've brought you some sustenance.'

She turned. 'I should be, I'm behind with this commission. But I keep thinking of what I've let myself in for, and it gets in the way.'

'Talking to Alex, you mean?'

She nodded, perching on her stool as she sipped the wine. 'I really like Roy, you know. He doesn't deserve this.'

Hugh lowered himself on to the chaise longue. 'You think it's her fault?'

'From what we've seen, don't you?'

'These things are usually six of one and half a dozen of the other.'

'Very profound, darling, but not a lot of help. If you ask me, all Roy has done is work hard and long, and not be available every time she lifts a finger. He obviously still dotes on her; when he snaps back, it's only in self-defence.'

'If you take that attitude, you won't get far with your sister,' Hugh commented astutely.

'She already knows it. The trouble is, when you fall out of love with someone they automatically start to irritate you. It's cruel, but a fact of life.'

'Oh, come now, you don't think it's that serious?'

'I'm beginning to wonder. Let's hope it's

99

only a temporary blip.'

Hugh was silent for a while, then he asked, 'What will you say to her?'

'Lord knows. She won't tell me anything she doesn't want to. She never has.'

'What about her friends? Could you approach one of them?'

'I don't think it would help. She has plenty, but I doubt if she confides in them. Amy Paxton was the exception, and she emigrated to Australia a couple of years ago. Alex still misses her.'

'Will you phone in advance, or just go round?'

'Drop in, I think. If she's warned, she might try to put me off.'

Hugh finished his wine and stood up. 'Are you coming down?'

'In a couple of minutes. I'll just tidy up here.'

He nodded, and went back downstairs. Gillian drained her glass and turned back to the easel, but her thoughts were still elsewhere. Sonia and Alex; she loved them both dearly, and both were unhappy. Furthermore, on Thursday they'd be here for dinner, with their respective husbands. Not, perhaps, such a good idea after all, but it was too late now to retract. The evening looked like being difficult, and Gillian felt her heart sink. Still, Hugh would back her up.

Bless him, she thought with a rush of

affection. How lucky she was to be able to depend on him so completely, confident that he would always be there to support her. If only all marriages could be like theirs. *And they lived happily ever after* really did seem a fairy tale these days.

But enough philosophizing, she told herself. Briskly she rinsed her brushes, wiped the palette and closed the paint box. Then, picking up her empty glass, she went downstairs.

CHAPTER SIX

Frederick was sorting out ideas for his talk when Paul Blake arrived the next morning. He swivelled in his chair as the younger man was shown in, and waved him to a seat.

'Damn nuisance, this,' he said, indicating the papers on his desk. 'I wish I'd never agreed to it. Much rather get down to work on the book.'

'Talking of which, I've typed up the notes you made in Canada.' Paul handed over a file.

'Thanks.' Frederick laid them on the desk on top of a pile of newspapers. 'I've been reading up on this blasted murder—it's sure to come up in the questions, and I should at least know what I'm talking about.'

'Well, this might help.' Paul took a large envelope out of his briefcase. 'It's a photo of

101

the victim, as requested. I managed to wheedle it out of a friend who works on the *News*.'

'Excellent man!' Frederick eagerly drew out the print and sat in silence for several minutes while his eyes moved slowly and assessingly over it. It showed a man in his mid forties, whose hair was already beginning to recede. The eyes were diffident, the mouth vulnerable, the chin rather weak. A very different character from Trevor Philpott.

'He looks pretty harmless,' he commented at last. 'I'm amazed he was capable of arousing such violence.'

'That's what struck me.'

'He's more the random-victim type, attacked in the course of robbery, for example. But we know that wasn't the case; he was specifically lured to his death. In heaven's name, why?'

Blake crossed his legs. 'I tried your trick with the photo, asking myself how he'd have struck me if I hadn't known anything about him.'

Frederick looked up interestedly. 'And?'

'I'd have said he was kindly, caring, possibly a little too anxious to please. Would you agree?'

'I suppose so, yes.'

'What occurred to me, though, is that people like that can be surprisingly stubborn if they think they're in the right. They hold to their opinions or course of action like terriers, and won't let go.'

'And you're suggesting one of those opinions or courses of action might have threatened the killer?'

'It's a possibility.'

'That's a very interesting thought, Paul. Did you by any chance go one step further, and come up with what it might be?'

Blake grinned. 'I'm afraid not. That's more your line—and the police's.'

When Frederick remained silent, still staring down at the photograph, he asked, 'Is there anything else you'd like me to do?'

'Not at the moment, thank you, but after tomorrow evening I'll start work in earnest. There's a slight problem, though; as you know, the first five cases corresponded with the breaking of the first five Commandments. But as we don't know the motive in the Philpott case, it follows that we don't know which broken Commandment lay behind it.'

Paul closed his briefcase. 'After speaking to his widow, which would you plump for? Adultery?'

'That, or coveting his neighbour's wife.' He thoughtfully tapped the photograph. 'I doubt whether either applied in Judd's case, though of course I could be wrong.'

'Thou shalt not be stubborn and hold to thine own opinions?' Paul suggested, getting to his feet.

'Go on with you! At least I don't need to

103

worry about him for the book, thank God. And don't forget I leave myself a loophole: I'm willing to concede that about five per cent of murders don't fit my theory. His could be one of those.'

'Good luck with the talk,' Paul said as he let himself out of the room.

Frederick merely grunted and returned to his papers.

*   *   *

'Oh—Gilly.'

Not the most enthusiastic of welcomes, but nor had she expected one.

'Hello, Alex. Any chance of a coffee?'

'Of course. Come in.'

Gillian followed her sister to the kitchen. 'Are the boys out?'

'When are they not?'

'Be thankful they don't need entertaining.' Gillian watched Alex as she prepared the coffee, noting the set of her shoulders, the way she held her head. Both indicated tension, but then she'd have guessed the purpose of the visit.

She came back to the table with two steaming mugs and sat down opposite Gillian. 'I suppose you've come to lecture me,' she said.

'No, to ask if there's any way I can help.'

'Help me behave better than I did

104

yesterday? I'm aware that I blotted my copybook.'

'Alex, what is it? Surely you can tell me?'

Her sister's outburst took her completely by surprise.

'How can I tell you?' Alex flared. 'Big sister, who's always done everything right? Life's been pretty uncomplicated for you, hasn't it? You sailed through exams, came top of the class at art school, married the year's most eligible bachelor, and built up a successful career, which just happens to be doing what you most enjoy. And to crown it all, as is patently obvious, you and Hugh are as much in love as the day you married. Probably more so. But it doesn't always work out like that.'

She fished for a handkerchief and angrily blew her nose.

'Oh, Alex, love, you've nothing to be defensive about. You've also got a husband who loves you, and two super kids—you've gone one better than me there! As for a career, you know you love working at the bookshop—it's even tailored to school holidays.'

Alex's face remained closed.

Gillian went on gently, feeling her way. 'There's something wrong, though, isn't there? I thought perhaps if we could talk it over, we might—'

'You,' Alex interrupted forcefully, 'are the last person I could talk to—or almost. No, don't look like that, I didn't mean—oh, what the hell.' She sat back in her chair and stared defiantly at her sister.

'I'm having an affair with Patrick Knowles. There—that's shocked you, hasn't it?'

Gillian gazed at her, eyes widening in disbelief. 'Oh, Alex, no!'

'Oh, Gilly, yes!'

'But—how? I thought you barely knew each other.'

'It started at the Country Club. One New Year kiss, and my goose was cooked. I can't even say I fought against it, because I didn't. Patrick's the most exciting thing that's happened to me for years. But there's no need to look so stricken—we don't intend to hurt anyone. We're not planning to run away or get divorced or anything. No one need ever know.'

'Sonia does already,' Gillian said flatly.

'What?'

'That there's someone else, I mean. And Roy's only too aware, from the way you've been behaving, that *something's* seriously wrong. If you think you can keep it quiet much longer, you're living in cloud-cuckoo-land.'

Gillian shook her head despairingly. 'Oh, Alex, how could you? To Sonia, of all people? She really doesn't deserve this.'

'Don't ask me to give him up, because I can't.'

'That's nonsense, and you know it.'

Alex smiled. 'You see, you *have* come to

106

lecture me.'

Gillian leant forward, taking one of her hands. 'Have you thought it through? It wouldn't be very pleasant being labelled The Other Woman, quite apart from the effect on Roy's career, and the boys having to face snide remarks at school.'

'It's not as though we're celebrities, for God's sake. Who cares what the hell we do?'

'Celebrities or not, the family's well-known in the town. Of course there'll be gossip. And just listen to yourself. You say you're not planning a divorce: analysed, that means you want to hold on to your marriage, while you continue to amuse yourself with Patrick. If you were really in love with him, that wouldn't be enough.'

Alex said slowly, 'Who said anything about love?'

Gillian drew a quavering breath. 'I see.'

'Animal instincts, sister dear. Not so pure and not so simple, but pretty basic. We just can't keep our hands off each other.' She gave an involuntary shudder.

'And you're prepared to risk everything for that?' Gillian asked incredulously. 'For something that, once the excitement wears off, will just fizzle out?'

Alex leaned forward, her voice low and intense. 'Look, Gilly, I don't *like* this any more than you do. It's an uncomfortable feeling, you know, not being in control of things. I *know* we're behaving badly and people might get hurt. I keep telling myself it's got to stop, but then when he—when we—'

'Forbidden fruits.'

'That's it, I suppose. The guilt adds to the excitement. And things had been getting a bit stale with Roy. Since his promotion he's working longer hours and away overnight quite often. And when he *is* home, he falls asleep in his chair! All the sparkle seemed to have gone out of life. You must admit Patrick Knowles is a dangerous man to meet in those circumstances, specially when the attraction is mutual.'

'Does he make a habit of it?' Gillian asked stiffly. 'Providing—sparkle—to jaded wives?'

'Don't be vile—of course not. He's always avoided married women up to now, and he'd not had anyone since he met Sonia.'

'Bully for him.'

Alex pushed back her chair. 'It's a waste of time trying to explain.'

Belatedly, Gillian remembered the purpose of her visit, to help rather than condemn. She was here, after all, as Alex's sister, not Sonia's friend.

'I'm sorry,' she said. 'I'm not trying to judge you, I'm just asking you to take stock and decide if this is how you want your life to be.'

'Not indefinitely, no.'

'Lord, make me good, but not yet?'

'Exactly,' Alex agreed, and had the grace to

smile. 'Oh, Gilly, I'm sorry I shocked you. I don't like myself very much at the moment, and you forced me to admit it. You won't tell Hugh about this, will you?'

'Not if you don't want me to. What about Roy? Do you still love him?'

'Of course I do,' Alex said impatiently. 'That's not the point.'

'I'd have thought it was very much the point.'

'Then you haven't understood anything. Look, Roy's part of my life, my husband and the father of my children. I can't imagine life without him.'

'You might have to,' Gillian said shortly.

'How do you mean?'

'What do you think he'll do, if—when—he finds out? Let you continue your fling with Patrick till you tire of it, then welcome you back with open arms? I shouldn't count on it.'

Alex said—but with less certainty—'He's not going to find out.'

'The longer the affair continues, the more likely it is.'

'That's blackmail!'

'No, just common sense. And you're all coming to dinner on Thursday, don't forget.'

'Perhaps we'd better drop out, in the circumstances.'

'Oh, no. I want you to see for yourself the state Sonia's in—but for God's sake don't wear your Chanel perfume.'

Alex stared at her, stricken. 'Is that how —?'

'One of the things. Look, Alex, I'm not trying to lecture you; all I'm asking is that you weigh up which is more important to you—all this'—she waved her hand to encompass the house and garden, symbolizing the status quo—'or a bit of forbidden excitement with someone who's cheating on his wife. And then take the appropriate action.'

'And here endeth what I sincerely hope is the last lesson.'

'Yes, it is, I promise. I've said all I want to say. The rest is up to you. Now I'll go and leave you in peace. Thanks for the coffee.'

Alex followed her to the front door and opened it. 'I suppose Roy asked you to speak to me?'

Gillian hesitated, then nodded. 'He's pretty desperate.'

'What will you tell him?'

'That you're going through a bit of a crisis, but you still love him. That's true, isn't it?'

Alex nodded. 'Thanks, Gilly.'

Gillian leant forward and kissed her. 'Be a good girl, little sister,' she said, 'and I'll see you at Pop's talk tomorrow.'

* * *

Webb spent most of that morning on paperwork. There were cases he'd been working on before the pub killing which still

110

needed his attention, and he'd temporarily pushed Judd to the back of his mind when the telephone rang and Harry Good's voice said in his ear, 'Geronimo!'

With his attention elsewhere, it took Webb a moment to identify the voice, let alone grasp its content. But as Harry continued talking, his brain slipped rapidly into gear.

'We've tracked down a Ford Escort matching the description given by the witness at the Nutmeg. Local garage says it fills up there from time to time, and one of the lads remembered doing an MOT on it a few months back. He went through the certificates, and there it was, complete with registration.'

'Excellent!' Webb said, as Good paused for breath. 'And the owner?'

'Swansea duly obliged: Lee Baring of Grange Road, Fallowfield. What's more, he's got form—mostly breaking and entering, though the last time he got five years for aggravated burglary. He was released a few months back after the usual remission.'

'Minor league, wouldn't you say? It hardly equates with premeditated murder. Have you brought him in?'

'That's where the good news runs out; at the moment, he's travelling round the country selling agricultural machinery.'

'Great! Don't his employers know where?'

'Only within a certain radius. He gets the business, so they allow him a bit of leeway as long as he rings in twice a week with orders and to report progress. The last call was from Cirencester on Friday.'

'When did he set off on this odyssey?'

'Tuesday, but the trip had been scheduled for some time.'

'All the same, he could have topped friend Judd before he went. The million-dollar question is, when's he due back?'

'Any day now. As I said, they don't monitor him too closely. As long as he achieves a steady turnover, they leave him to his own devices.'

'Did they want to know why we're interested?'

'No, we took the precaution of using one of the women officers; without anything specific being said, they assumed she was a girlfriend.'

'Is he married, this Baring?'

'Was last time we had dealings with him, but there's no one at the house. Susie didn't ask, since a girlfriend would have known.'

'So it's back to the waiting game. Sounds promising, all the same. Thanks, Harry; keep me in touch.'

Webb replaced his phone and sat for a moment, tapping his pen on the desk. Then, with a sigh, he turned back to the less interesting papers that awaited him.

*　　　*　　　*

'Hannah?' It was Gwen. 'Are you by any chance free this afternoon?'

Since Hannah's plans had progressed no further than a book and a cold drink in the garden, she admitted that she was.

'I've had a chance now to go through the things you left for me, and I think it's time we had a discussion.'

Hannah sighed. After a strenuous year standing in as headmistress, she was still revelling in the freedom of the summer holidays, and the thought of having to turn her mind back to school matters held no appeal. Still, they obviously needed to talk sometime, and perhaps the sooner the better, while it was all relatively fresh in her mind.

'Certainly, Gwen. I'll come over, shall I?'

'If you would. About two-thirty?'

'See you then.' Hannah scooped up the marmalade cat which, while she'd been talking, had appropriated her chair. She held him for a moment, rubbing her face against his silky fur and listening to his deep-throated purr. Then she reseated herself, settled him on her lap, and picked up the local paper which she'd been reading when the phone rang.

The Arts Page was devoted to the Broadshire Festival of Literature, with a list of venues and the eminent speakers who would be taking part. In one of the boxes, under the heading 'Ashmartin Central Library', she read: *Tuesday 30th July. Mr Frederick Mace, the well-*

known writer and criminologist, will be speaking on 'Murder Under the Microscope' at 8 pm. Tickets £5 to include a glass of wine and canapés.

That, she reflected, might be interesting. Perhaps he would expand on some of the ideas he'd mentioned on television. Also, while David could hardly go to the talk himself, she might learn something of interest on his behalf.

The decision taken, Hannah laid aside the paper and picked up pen and pad to make notes for her discussion with Gwen.

*   *   *

The house had lost its musty smell, but in the sitting-room there was the unmistakable scent of old age. Hannah, shown in there on her arrival, chatted for a minute or two with Mrs Rutherford, happily restored to her own armchair after almost a year with her elder daughter.

'There's nothing quite like your own,' she commented contentedly. 'Beatrice and John couldn't have been kinder, but as the song says, there's no place like home.'

Hannah smiled across at Gwen, and surprised an expression on her face that she couldn't interpret. Then it was gone, and Gwen said briskly, 'Well, if you'll excuse us, Mother, we'll move to the dining-room and get down to business. We'll join you for a cup of tea later.'

The dining-room was at the front of the house, and from its open window sounds from the park reached them sporadically as they worked. To her dismay, Hannah found she was becoming increasingly irritated as, one after another, the modest innovations she'd introduced over the last year were systematically ruled out. Gwen made no particular criticism of them; it was more a case of, 'I can't see that would be much advantage,' or, 'Well, now that I'm back—'

Once, Hannah was stung to interject, 'Actually, it worked very well. The girls—'

But Gwen, smiling vaguely, had moved on to the next point, and Hannah's annoyance slowly deepened to anger. It was so totally unexpected; she and Gwen had worked admirably together for years, in almost total harmony. As long, Hannah thought with a flash of insight, as Gwen was head and she herself mere deputy. And she realized, again with a small shock, that Gwen, though she'd rather die than admit it, resented the efficiency Hannah had shown while she'd been away.

She was still coming to terms with that when she realized uncomfortably that there was another side to the coin: Gwen's attitude had brought home to her just how much she'd enjoyed running the school herself, implementing new ideas and being free—

within reason—to direct things in the way she considered best.

It did not help that during all this negating of her ideas, Gwen had made no comment on Hannah's safe handling of the school through what she knew to have been a far from easy year. Hannah found herself wondering with asperity how Gwen would have handled the suicide of a member of staff, the insidious spread of a dangerous cult, the scandal which drove a school governor to take his life.

She had always known that behind the flapping, disorganized exterior, there was a ruthless streak in Gwen which ensured that she got her own way. It was simply that this ruthlessness had never before been directed at her, and she did not enjoy the experience.

Having disposed of everything Hannah had initiated, Gwen moved on to what was obviously the main reason for their meeting— the changes she herself wished to implement, based on her experience of the Canadian system.

Some, Hannah mentally dismissed as scarcely worth incorporating—no doubt as Gwen had viewed her own. Others she conceded might be an improvement, but there were several major changes that she was convinced would be wrong for Ashbourne.

'Don't you see the upsets they'd cause?' she asked urgently. 'The governors would never accept them, let alone the parents.'

116

'I'm quite confident of bringing them round. Unlike the rest of you, I've had the advantage of seeing them in operation.'

'But Canada's very different from England, Gwen. The whole system is. It just wouldn't work here.'

Gwen fixed her with eyes that were no longer either shy or diffident. 'Don't you think I should be the judge of that?'

Hannah forced a smile. 'Well, don't let's argue about it. We can bring it up at the next board meeting and see what the reaction is.'

'Of course.' Gwen closed the file in front of her. 'But I wanted to talk it over with you first, as a matter of courtesy.'

'I appreciate that.'

There was a pause as they regarded one another, each aware of the shift in their relationship and uncertain how to deal with it. Then Gwen said in half-apology, 'A year's a long time, Hannah. It will take me a while to settle back into things.'

'I know; that's why I feel it would be as well to take things slowly.'

'We'll see. Now, if you'd like to go and rejoin Mother, I'll put the kettle on.'

*   *   *

That evening, Hannah tried to explain her worries to Webb. 'The awful thing is, we're not comfortable with each other any more. It's

117

almost as though we don't trust each other.'

'A year's a long time,' Webb said, unconsciously echoing Gwen. 'You're bound to have grown apart a little. Things will ease next term, when you're back in harness again.'

Hannah said reflectively, 'It'll be hard for me too, having been in charge for a year. I'm surprised how much I mind the prospect of stepping down.'

'But you always knew it was temporary,' Webb reminded her.

'Somehow, that doesn't help! And she did go on, David. Even during tea, everything was Canada this and Canada that. I felt like asking why she'd bothered to come home!'

'Obviously she's full of it, after being out there so long,' he pointed out reasonably. 'Give her time. Keep out of her way for a while and let things die down.'

'But suppose we can't regain our old footing? It would make things very awkward.'

'I still think you're jumping the gun. Relax; you've got about six weeks of holiday ahead of you. I wish I had your problems!'

Hannah laughed. 'Sorry, but I needed to get that off my chest. All right, I promise not to bring it up again. Tell me how the inquiry's going.'

So he told her about the elusive Lee Baring and the watch being kept on his house.

'If he's the villain, there should be no difficulty nailing him—there are bound to be traces in the car. And once we have that under our belts, we can sound him out on the Feathers case.'

'But there's no doubt, is there? It's virtually an identical crime.'

'On the face of it, yes, but that's not conclusive. Still, it would be a terrific bonus if we could tie them both up at the same time.'

'Which reminds me, I'm going to Ashmartin tomorrow evening, to hear Frederick Mace.'

'Again? His publicity agent's working overtime.'

'Well, he's a local celebrity and it's the Broadshire Festival of Literature, in case you hadn't noticed.'

Webb grinned. 'I admit it had escaped me.'

'I thought he might come up with something interesting that I could pass on to you.'

'I'm not sure how to take that,' he protested. 'I like to think we're capable of solving our own crimes, without depending on academic old gentlemen!'

'All right, be like that, but *I* want to hear him.'

'Mind you don't break any Commandments,' Webb said, and ducked as Hannah threw a cushion at him.

'Anyway,' she finished, 'perhaps by tomorrow evening, Mr Baring will be behind bars, and that will be an end of it.'

119

CHAPTER SEVEN

Inquiries had established that Bill Price, nominated by Mrs Judd as her husband's closest friend, worked as a clerk in the National Bank in Dominion Street. Webb and Jackson were shown into a private room and minutes later Price himself appeared, a tall, thin man with a stoop and an unsuccessful moustache.

Webb waved him to one of his own—or at least the bank's—chairs.

'We understand from his wife that you were a friend of Simon Judd,' he began.

'Yes, that's right.' Price spoke quickly, as though eager to be of help. 'A terrible thing—quite unbelievable. Old Simon wasn't the type to get himself murdered.'

Webb's mouth twitched. 'I wasn't aware there was a "type".'

'Well, you know what I mean. He'd not a wrong word to say about anybody. He was just an ordinary, decent chap going about his business and trying to pull his weight in the community.'

St Simon. Like St Trevor in Oxbury. Damn it, both men must have had some faults; this was carrying not speaking ill of the dead too far.

'How well did you know him, sir?'

120

'As well as anyone, I'd say. Since schooldays.'

'Would you say his marriage was happy?'

'Good Lord, yes. He wasn't a womanizer, if that's what you're wondering. In fact, he was so shy we wondered if he'd ever pluck up the courage to propose to Ella.'

'We?'

'Me and his other pals.'

'Who were they?'

'Keith Denham, Mark Scott and Bob Naylor. We used to go round in a crowd at one time, then we lost touch. Keith moved away, Mark works on the continent, and Bob just seemed to drop out of sight.'

'What about more recently?' Webb inquired. 'Who was Judd friendly with at the time of his death?' He'd had no luck with Judd's wife on that question, perhaps some names would emerge now.

But Price was shaking his head. 'As I said, I knew him as well as anyone, but I wouldn't say we were close. Simon got on with everyone, but he kept himself to himself. Even when we were lads, swopping experiences with girls, Si would listen to the rest of us, but he'd never volunteer anything. Come to think of it, maybe that's why he was good at his job—just listening.'

'Can you recall his having an argument with anyone, disagreeing with something someone had done?'

'I wouldn't call them arguments, but he had strong principles and he stuck to them.'

'What kind of principles?'

'Well, that you should be punished if you did something wrong. That kind of thing. Funny, really; a lot of people think social workers are too soft by half—do-gooders—but Simon wasn't like that. He'd move heaven and earth to help someone in trouble, but if they'd done wrong, he thought they ought to take the consequences.'

Interesting, Webb thought. 'Any particular instances?'

'Can't think of one offhand, but it was always general stuff, something in the papers or on the news. He never talked about his work.'

Unlikely, then, to be of much relevance. All the same, the conversation had given a slightly different slant on Simon Judd. Had he stuck to his principles once too often? It was an angle which might warrant investigation.

As they came out on to the street, Webb saw a notice advertising Frederick Mace's talk that evening and, despite his comments to Hannah, felt a flicker of interest. The old boy was pretty astute; would he consider that Judd's judgemental qualities strengthened or weakened his theory of broken Commandments?

Shrugging aside such hypotheses, Webb reached for his mobile to check if there'd been any sighting yet of Baring.

*　　　*　　　*

Patrick Knowles steered the car on to the verge and drew to a halt. As the engine died, silence enfolded him, broken only by the distant hum of a plane, almost invisible in the summer sky. Ahead and behind, the country road stretched emptily, shimmering in the heat-haze.

He had twenty minutes before his next appointment, and was glad of a breathing space. Life was becoming altogether too complicated; only a few months ago, he'd been happily cruising along, with no problems of any consequence. Now, a host of them buzzed in his head, battling for supremacy. Unfastening his seat belt, he wound down the window and settled back, drumming his fingers restlessly on the steering wheel.

High on the list, as always, came his mother and sister. Neither was strong, and recently both seemed to be deteriorating. Zoë was increasingly nervy, making him fear the onset of another breakdown, while his mother's health, uncertain for years, was now failing rapidly. The time was fast approaching when she would be too much for Zoë to cope with on her own. Then what? He hated the idea of a nursing home, but if it did become necessary, what would happen to his sister?

123

Common sense dictated that she should move in with them, but since she and Sonia barely tolerated each other, it would not make for a congenial household.

Sonia. Another of his worries, though admittedly of his own making. The trouble was that his affair with Alex had got completely out of hand. How the hell could he have known, when he gave her that New Year kiss, that it would light such a fuse between them? Even thinking of her now aroused him. He reached for the car phone and dialled her number.

'Hello?'

'It's me. Can you talk?'

'Briefly—the twins are in the garden.'

'Any chance of seeing you today?'

'Not when the boys are home, Patrick. You know that.'

'How about this evening? Invent someone you have to visit!'

He heard her low laugh. 'Afraid I can't; we're all going to the library for Pop's talk. Still, I'll see you on Thursday.'

'With Sonia, Roy and your sister. Wonderful.'

'Patrick—' There was a hesitant note in her voice.

'What?'

'I think we should go carefully for a while. Sonia told Gilly she thinks you're seeing someone.'

He drew in his breath, eyes narrowing.

'When was this?'

'Last week, I think. She doesn't know who, though.'

'Then why did your sister mention it?'

Silence.

His voice sharpened. 'Alex?'

She said quietly, 'I told her. About us.'

'God, are you out of your mind? When she and Sonia are so close? Whatever possessed you to —?'

'She came round to see if she could help.'

'What do you mean?'

'I snapped at Roy during the family lunch, and he despatched Gilly to find out what was wrong.'

'And you told her!'

'Oh, she won't pass it on; you needn't worry about that.'

'But *she* knows, damn it, and she'll be watching us like a hawk on Thursday. Sonia's bound to notice. God, what a mess.'

'So what do we do? Stop seeing each other altogether?'

'Is that what you want?' he demanded harshly, and heard her sigh.

'No, not yet. Do you?'

'You know damn well I don't. God, Alex—'

'Yes,' she said softly, 'I know. I know. But we never meant to hurt anyone, did we? If it's going to cause—'

'We'll just have to be more careful, as you said. You stop snapping at Roy and I'll tread

125

carefully with Sonia. God knows how she latched on to anything, I didn't think I'd been any different.'

'I must go—Jack's calling.'

'Till Thursday, then.'

'Bye.'

The line went dead and he switched off the phone. The call had been intended as an antidote to his problems; instead, it had merely added to them. He refastened his seat belt, started up the car and drove on to his appointment.

* * *

Hannah had invited her friend, Dilys Hayward, to accompany her to the talk. A writer herself, Dilys had in fact already participated in the Festival of Literature—with a talk at Shillingham Library—but she was eager to hear Frederick Mace, and Hannah arranged to collect her at seven-fifteen.

'This should be interesting,' she commented, settling into the car. 'I saw him on TV the other evening; a fascinating man.'

'He came to the school a few years ago,' Hannah said.

'Talking of school, I hear Gwen's back?'

Dilys and Hannah had been contemporaries at Ashbourne, Gwen some five years their senior. Though the gap had been insurmountable during schooldays, in latter years the women—all unmarried and successful in their careers—had become friends and met regularly for dinner or the theatre. Monica Tovey, Gwen's contemporary, had been a fourth until her recent marriage to the local bank manager.

'That's right; I went there for tea yesterday.'

'And?' Dilys prompted.

'We went through everything that's happened while she's been away.'

'I meant, how was she? Has she changed at all?'

'Yes,' Hannah said slowly, 'I rather think she has. Either that, or I have. Perhaps a bit of both.'

'Oh dear.'

'I suppose we're bound to be a bit constrained with each other after so long.'

'And you did have one hell of a year,' Dilys said feelingly, remembering her own encounter with the religious cult which had threatened the school. When Hannah made no comment, she added, 'How was she different?'

'Well, for one thing, she never stopped singing Canada's praises. I'd had quite enough of it by the end of the afternoon, I can tell you. What's more, she wants to introduce all kinds of things they do over there which I'm convinced wouldn't transplant.

'It wasn't only that, though,' Hannah went on, negotiating the traffic as they joined the main Ashmartin road. 'She seemed different in

127

herself. If I had to define it, I'd say she was unhappy.'

'Probably culture shock, coming back to dear old Mum after all the bright lights.'

Hannah laughed. 'That might well be it. No doubt she'll settle down.'

'I must give her a ring,' Dilys said. 'I can't believe it's a year since I saw her.'

'Tell you what, I'll try to fix a dinner later in the week, then you can judge for yourself. I'll see if Monica's free, too. It'll be like old times.'

Ashmartin Central Library had a car park at the rear, and they managed to secure one of the last spaces. 'Just as well I reserved our tickets,' Hannah commented, 'it seems to be a popular event.'

They walked round the modern building, its golden stone glowing in the evening sunlight, and through the open double doors. The library itself lay behind a glass wall to the left, but the man who took their tickets directed them upstairs for 'refreshments', where they found themselves engulfed in a milling throng.

As they stood hesitating, a girl came forward with a tray of red and white wine and soft drinks. Hannah and Dilys each selected a glass and moved to the long trestle tables where a selection of sausage rolls, slices of quiche and canapés was laid out.

Hannah, turning away with her plate, surveyed the crowd around her, noting that they were a varied cross-section. There was the expected sprinkling of academics, earnest young men and women in long cardigans despite the heat, some with glasses perched on their noses and all clutching notebooks.

There was a proportion of local residents, conscientiously supporting their library; and there was a section which Hannah suspected, possibly unjustly, of being sensation-seekers: people who would not ordinarily have crossed the street to hear Frederick Mace, but who had either seen his television interview or—more likely—heard about it afterwards, and hoped to learn something more of the local murder. But among all the varied crowd, she didn't see one face she recognized.

Eventually someone rang a handbell and raised his voice above the babble of conversation. 'Ladies and gentlemen, if you'd like to make your way downstairs and take your seats, Mr Mace will begin his talk.'

Hannah and Dilys moved with the flow down the wide staircase and through the now open doors into the library, which was set out with rows of chairs forming a semicircle. In front of them was a table and chair and over to one side, another table bearing several piles of books, guarded by a representative from Mace's publishers.

The audience settled itself expectantly and Frederick Mace appeared from one of the aisles of books, escorted by the chief librarian, who proceeded to introduce him.

Hannah only half listened, her eyes on Mace. He was tall and narrow-shouldered and wore his clothes comfortably, like a man not unduly concerned with his appearance. He had, she thought, an interesting, lived-in face. There were heavy grooves down his cheeks and slight pouches under the eyes. The eyes themselves, narrow and grey, were sharp but kindly, and he was fortunate enough to have kept his hair, which had a slight wave and was a dark iron grey.

The theme of the talk, as its title implied, was his work as a criminologist, and—possibly mindful of his publisher—he made frequent reference to his book, *The Muddied Pool*, which had been the subject of his tour. Hannah surreptitiously removed a notebook from her handbag and jotted down a few points, as much for her own interest as David's. Mace was obviously a seasoned speaker; he did not talk down to his audience, but stated his findings and made his deductions in clear, easily understood language rather than the scientific jargon frequently heard in that context. There was genuine and enthusiastic applause as he came to an end. The chief librarian stood up briefly to thank him, and to invite questions from the audience.

'Here we go,' murmured Dilys under her breath, as several hands shot up.

At Mace's nod, a man a few rows behind

them stood up. 'Mr Mace, I'm sure many of us saw your interview on television last week, and were fascinated by your Ten Commandments theory. I wonder if you'd enlarge on that for us, especially with regard to murder?'

There were several murmurs of agreement.

Frederick Mace shifted on his chair—uncomfortably, Hannah thought, though he must have known this was coming. 'Well, as I mentioned in my interview, murder is, of course, the ultimate crime, but other, possibly lesser, ones frequently lead to it.'

'Making the victim partially responsible, you mean?' asked the questioner, who had remained standing.

'In some cases, possibly; in others, it is a third party who has, either wilfully or inadvertently, set the thing in train. Because in most cases, the murderer has a motive for his crime, and it follows there must be grounds for that motive, whether real or imaginary—something which has ignited his hatred of that particular person. It can often be traced to the prior breaking of a Commandment.'

Another member of the audience, a woman in the second row, raised her hand and simultaneously stood up. 'Could you tell us, Mr Mace, how this ties in with the two pub murders?'

He steepled his fingers and regarded them for a moment. 'You must understand that anything I say is pure hypothesis. I'm not privy

131

to police cogitations, nor have I anything to go on other than my own observation. However, having now read a considerable amount about both cases, I do not believe, however closely they might resemble each other, that these crimes were committed from the same motive.'

There was a stirring of interest, an excited whispering which spread through the audience and was immediately stifled.

'To illustrate my point,' Mace continued, 'let us look not at the similarities between the murders, but at the differences, and these, I suggest, are apparent not only with regard to the murderer—who, in each case, appears to be the telephone caller—but also to the victims.

'Let's take the victims first: I never met either of them, but I've studied their photographs, and from these, together with reports I've read in the press, it appears they were very different types. Mr Philpott was jovial, self-confident, perhaps a little boastful—a typical salesman, you might think. Mr Judd, on the other hand, was much quieter, shy but with, I suspect, an underlying strength. A dedicated social worker, he was essentially an intensely private man.

'When we come to the killer, we have to rely on those phone calls, and fortunately we have descriptions of the voice in each case. Mr Philpott's caller was well spoken, with a fairly deep tone—perhaps not unlike Mr Philpott

132

himself. At any rate, the girl on the switchboard warmed to him. I spoke to her personally, and she told me he'd sounded "nice".

'On the other hand, according to the press, Mr Judd's killer had a much lighter voice with a slight local accent, and it was described as "shaky".

'I might be entirely wrong, but I'd deduce from this that in the first instance the murderer was out to avenge someone else— someone close to him but at one remove, as it were, which enabled him to retain his self-control. In the second, he felt himself so deeply and personally involved that he couldn't conceal his emotions. This, mind you, despite the fact that Judd recognized neither his voice nor his appearance. How, I ask myself, could Judd have done him so great a wrong "long-distance"?

'And this is what intrigues me most of all— the fact that each man spoke directly to his killer, *but neither of them recognized his voice.* Nor, one must assume, his appearance; because if, despite the probably false name, the caller turned out to be someone the victim had met, he'd immediately have become suspicious and not got trustingly into the car with him. I'm therefore forced to conclude that neither victim was known personally to his killer, which, since both murders were premeditated, I find fascinating.

'Obviously, some murders *are* motiveless, committed merely for the sake of killing, and such victims are picked at random. But in both these cases he was asked for by name, and I believe the killer had a strong personal reason—or at least thought he had—for committing murder.'

Frederick Mace paused and surveyed his audience. 'However,' he went on into the expectant silence, 'I do not believe it was the same reason, *nor the same killer.*'

There was a collective gasp from the audience, followed by a buzz of conversation.

'Well, go on, lad!' someone called from the back. 'You can't leave it there!' And tension was released in a spontaneous burst of laughter.

'Very well, but again I emphasize this is purely my own opinion. The difference between the voices is not, of course, conclusive; since it could have been disguised, it would be necessary to test each call scientifically, which, since they obviously weren't recorded, is impossible.

'But another consideration is the fact that if the same man *was* responsible for both cases, he'd be on the way to becoming a serial killer. And serial killers tend either to go for the same kind of person—prostitutes, for instance, or young boys—or kill from the same motive. Which, as I've explained, does not apply here.'

He looked at the rapt faces in front of him,

and smiled mischievously. 'I rest my case!' he said.

'So which Commandments would you say had been broken?' someone called, but Frederick Mace had had enough.

He smilingly shook his head. 'I think we should leave it there. I've waffled on quite long enough.' His eyes twinkled. 'And we must leave the police *something* to do, after all!'

The questioner made one last attempt. 'But couldn't you just —?'

The chief librarian cut him off. 'Ladies and gentlemen, Mr Mace has been more than generous, giving us so much of his time. We must allow him to stop now. I'm sure you'd like to know he'll be happy to sign copies of his book, which is available over here.' He gestured towards the publisher and her table. 'And now, please will you show your appreciation for such an interesting and informative talk.'

'I'm going to buy a copy,' Hannah said, under the storm of applause, 'though I confess I'll be more interested in the next one.'

'An intriguing theory,' Dilys acknowledged, 'but I'm sure the police would find flaws in it.'

Hannah smiled without replying. She would shortly find out. She rose and threaded her way past the others in their row towards the book table, where already a queue was forming.

A few people had now joined Frederick

135

Mace—his family, presumably. Hannah studied them with interest. His wife was a fairly small woman, sensible-looking, with short brown hair and a clear skin unembellished by make-up, but the two younger women—daughters? daughters-in-law?—were very attractive, one fair and one dark. Their husbands, seemingly unwilling to step into the spotlight, stood awkwardly to one side, conversing with each other.

When it came to her turn for the signing, Hannah said, 'It was a fascinating talk, Mr Mace, thank you.'

He looked up with an automatic smile, then his expression sharpened. 'Haven't we met? Surely—'

'How clever of you—yes. I'm Hannah James, deputy head of Ashbourne. You came to speak to us.'

'Of course—I remember. Good to see you again, Miss James. Have you met my wife?' Hannah smilingly shook her hand. 'And my daughters, Gillian and Alexandra.' The two younger women dutifully came forward.

Hannah murmured something appropriate, smiled again, and, conscious of the lengthening queue behind her, moved away.

Dilys was waiting for her by the door. 'Let's make a move before there's a crush in the car park.' She glanced sideways at Hannah as they walked round the building. 'Why this sudden interest in crime?'

'Not so much crime, as the psychology behind it—what makes people criminals. Surely the more we understand it, the more hope we have of preventing it.'

She unlocked the car and Dilys slid inside. 'It will be interesting,' she commented, fastening her seat belt, 'to see in due course if he's proved right.'

*   *   *

Back at Beechcroft Mansions, Hannah took the lift to the floor beyond her own and knocked at Webb's door.

'Come in!' he greeted her. 'How was the oracle?'

'Thought provoking; I bought a copy of his book. Would you like to borrow it?'

'You reckon I need it?'

She smiled. 'No, I didn't mean that. It was an excellent talk, but, as you'd imagine, it was the Commandment business the audience really wanted to hear about.'

While he poured a drink she went to the window, leaning on the sill and looking down the long hill to the town nestling at its foot, shimmering with lights. It was a superb view from this height, especially in daylight, when the Chantock Hills were just discernible. The outlook from her own windows at the back of the house gave only on to the gardens.

'So,' Webb said, joining her with two glasses

137

and motioning her to a chair, 'what did he come up with?'

'About the pub murders? Basically, that there are two different killers with two different motives.'

'Wonderful.'

'You were hoping to tie them to one person?'

'It would have made life simpler. What grounds had he for that deduction?'

'It was mainly based on the telephone voices, which certainly seemed different, and on the victims' photographs.'

'*Photographs?*'

'He said a serial killer would have gone for the same type, and these two weren't. That, as you'll appreciate, is an oversimplification.'

'If he's right, we've precious little hope of catching Philpott's killer. All the stops were pulled out at the time, to no avail, and the trail's stone cold now.'

'What about the latest one?'

'We're still waiting for this Baring chap to show up. Bloody frustrating, hanging around not knowing when he's going to put in an appearance. According to his office he's now overdue.'

'Perhaps they told him you were making inquiries.'

'They were asked not to, but you never know. If he doesn't turn up tomorrow, we'll put out an All Ports Warning.'

Hannah stared into her glass. 'Mr Mace underlined the fact that neither Philpott nor Judd seemed to know their killers. He thinks Philpott was murdered by someone "at one remove", as he put it, that is, acting on behalf of another person.'

Webb raised a sceptical eyebrow. 'The crystal-ball syndrome. And Judd?'

'By someone who thought he'd done him a personal wrong, despite the fact that Judd didn't recognize him. Mace wondered how such a deep injury had been committed "long-distance".'

Webb took a mouthful of whisky. 'Well, he's been spot-on in the past, but to be frank, this sounds like a lot of baloney.'

'He did stress they were only theories.'

'So I should hope, and believe me we need more than theories. We're over a week into this now, and only the elusive Baring on the horizon. Or not even there.'

'But you had registered the voices on the phone were different?'

Webb said irritably, 'Of course we bloody registered it, but there's such a thing as disguising your voice, you know. We may even have an actor on our hands. Did your precious Mr Mace consider that?'

Hannah forbore from confirming that he had. She said softly, 'David, I'm sorry. I didn't mean to ram him down your throat. I thought you'd be interested, that's all.'

He reached out a hand and pulled her to him. 'No, I'm the one to apologize. Of course I'm interested, but all the theories in the world won't nail this bastard without some proof to back them up.'

'I know.' She nestled into his arms. 'Something'll break soon, I'm sure.'

'This crystal-gazing must be catching!' But he was smiling as he put his glass down on the table. 'And now let's talk about something much more interesting. Or, better still, not talk at all.'

CHAPTER EIGHT

The talk made the national papers the next morning, with an accompanying photograph of Frederick which appeared on his dust jackets.

BROADSHIRE PUB MURDERS NOT CONNECTED, SAYS CRIMINOLOGIST was a typical headline.

'This isn't going to endear Pop to the police,' Gillian commented a little anxiously over breakfast.

'Or to the killers,' Hugh added.

'So you do think there are two?'

'I'd say he proved that pretty conclusively, wouldn't you?'

'I don't know which is worse, having a serial killer on the loose, or two separate ones.'

'Well, from your father's angle it's all good

publicity.'

'He hates it, though. You know how he loathes discussing the book he's working on.'

'Not this time, apparently.'

'He didn't *want* to talk about it,' Gillian protested. 'They just didn't leave him any option.'

'Oh, I don't know; I reckon airing it all in public crystallized his ideas; he'll be raring to go this morning, you mark my words.' Hugh looked at his watch, and stood up.

'I hope you're right—and I also hope *he* is. He stated his opinion very publicly; I'd hate to see him proved wrong.'

Hugh bent to kiss her. 'Don't worry, my love, he's a tough old bird. Criticism runs off him like water off a duck's back. He wouldn't have survived this long if it didn't. I must go. What are you doing today?'

'I suppose I'll have to shop for the dinner party.'

'Anyone would think you weren't looking forward to it!' Gillian forced a smile and, as the front door closed behind him, refilled her coffee cup. She *wasn't* looking forward to the dinner party, but she couldn't admit it to Hugh since he didn't know about the Alex-Patrick-Sonia triangle. Though for how much longer it could be kept secret, she had no idea.

*   *   *

141

DI Crombie dropped a folded newspaper on Webb's desk, and the craggy face of Frederick Mace stared up at him.

'This man is beginning to haunt me,' he complained, running his eye down the column, which was more or less a recap of what Hannah had told him.

'Think he's right?'

'Lord knows. Just wheel in Lee Baring and I might give you an answer. Where the devil is he, Alan?'

The phone rang and Webb lifted it.

'Harry here, Dave. There's good news and bad news.'

'Let's hear it, then.'

'Baring was spotted leaving the M4 at the Ashmartin exit. He accelerated when he saw the patrol car, and they only caught up with him on the outskirts of town.' Good paused, then ended flatly: 'But before they could nab him, he was out of the car and had disappeared into a housing estate.'

'Brilliant.'

'The area's been sealed off and we're doing a house-to-house, but he almost certainly got clear.'

Webb said heavily, 'And the good news?'

'Well, we *have* got the car. SOCO are already working on it.'

'Does it fit the witness's description?'

'To a "t". Light-coloured Escort, faulty brake light, plastic sun visor, the lot.'

'Well, that's something. I'll look in later—there might be news by then. In the meantime I've put inquiries in hand concerning some old friends of Judd's, whose names I was given yesterday. It's a long shot, but it might pay off.'

Good's grunt reached him over the wire. 'With luck, we should be able to scrub the long shots. My money's on Baring. All we've got to do now is find him.'

*   *   *

Frederick sat at his desk, staring at the sheet of paper in front of him. At the top he'd written in his cramped hand: *Thou shalt not killl/commit adultery/covet thy neighbour's wife.* Which, as he was only too ready to admit, completely fudged the issue. Still, it was logical to turn to the Philpott case next, while it was so much in the news and he'd just met the widow. It could be slotted into the appropriate place once he'd settled on the most likely motive.

He frowned suddenly, wondering if Aileen Bradburn had, as he'd advised, notified the police of Philpott's affairs. It could give them a much-needed new lead—though not, he remained convinced, to the killer of Simon Judd.

He looked up the note he'd made when Paul gave him her number, pulled the phone towards him, and dialled it, resolving also to

143

ask for 'Jerry's' surname and address; it would do no harm to contact him, both about the women and the cricket club incident. But the ringing sound continued unanswered, and eventually, frustrated, he hung up. He'd try again later.

Propping the photograph of Trevor Philpott in front of him, he stared at it morosely. Why had he died? Which of his conquests had proved to have a jealous husband? Or had none of them?

Frederick opened the file of notes which Paul had typed up following his research, and began to read through it. He was interrupted by the phone.

'Mr Mace? Dick Thomson, Radio Broadshire *Current News*. I wonder if you'd be prepared to do an interview for us tomorrow morning?'

Frederick said gruffly, 'I've nothing further to say.'

'Actually, there are several angles we'd like to explore, especially regarding—'

'I'm sorry,' Frederick interrupted. 'I shan't be doing any more interviews for the moment. Goodbye.'

He put down the phone, feeling ungracious. But, Lord knew, he had to draw the line somewhere. At this rate, his whole time would be spent rushing from one place to another and he'd never get any work done.

Determinedly closing his mind to all else, he

returned to Paul's notes.

*   *   *

Edwina was uneasy, and, as always when something was worrying her, she had donned her gardening clothes and gone out to attack the weeds. In retrospect, she thought, the Canadian tour seemed like a holiday, where their only concern was to be ready for the limousine to conduct them from one venue, hotel or airport to the next.

She took out the secateurs and began methodically to deadhead the roses. It was very hot in this corner of the garden, and the sweet, heady scent of the flowers mingled with that of warm earth and the dusty brick wall alongside. In the full glare of the sun, Edwina was grateful for her old straw hat.

Snipping her way along the bed, she mentally lined up her worries for consideration.

First, of course, Alex. The atmosphere at Sunday lunch had been most uncomfortable, and she was as much concerned for Roy and the children as for her daughter. Gilly had said she'd go and see her, but with all the milling about at the talk last night, she'd not had the chance to ask the outcome.

She sighed, dropping the faded blooms into the trug. She loved her younger daughter dearly, but Alex had always been headstrong

145

and inclined to ride roughshod over anyone who obstructed her. In, of course, Edwina added smilingly to herself, the nicest possible way. For the first time, she wondered whether there was more to Alex and Roy's difficulties than she'd realized. Could one of them, for instance, have met someone else?

She straightened, rubbing her back as she gazed, eyes narrowed against the sun, down the length of the garden, considering the possibility. If so, it was unlikely to be Roy; he obviously still adored her. But Alex? Could she have become involved, without one of them noticing?

Edwina gave herself a little shake and returned to her deadheading. She was letting her imagination run away with her. Lots of marriages went through difficult patches; they would sort themselves out. But, added a niggling little voice in her head, lots more *didn't* sort themselves out; one heard of so many breaking down nowadays. She couldn't bear that to happen to Alex and Roy.

She'd ring Gilly this evening and find out how she'd got on. Meanwhile, her mind moved to another, more recent, worry, centred on Frederick. Basically, she did not care for the way he had suddenly been thrust into the limelight of this latest murder. It was fine to discuss, as he had in Canada, the theories outlined in his last book. Even the new one— though she'd been surprised he was prepared

146

to talk about it—as long as the crimes concerned were safely solved and in the past.

But why, oh why, had he admitted that he'd chosen the Feathers case for examination?

The television interview, the widespread press coverage, the library talk—all had combined to push him to the forefront of people's minds, synonymous with both the local murders. Suppose the killer decided he'd more to fear from Frederick than from the police?

In the fierce heat, Edwina gave a little shiver. All at once, she'd had enough of the empty, silent garden and her own thoughts. She'd go inside and have a glass of the lemonade she kept in the fridge. Then she'd prepare some salad and wash the strawberries for supper.

With everyday matters once more restoring the balance, she retrieved the trug, and set off purposefully towards the house.

*　　　*　　　*

It was late afternoon by the time Webb and Jackson reached the Ashmartin garage where SOCO were working on Baring's car. The senior man, seeing them standing in the doorway, came across.

'Anything worthwhile?' Webb asked, holding up his warrant card.

'The interior'd been given a pretty thorough

cleaning, but we found traces of blood, both in the rubber mat on the passenger side and on the back of the seat. There were also samples under the driver and passenger seats—hairs, fibres, blades of grass.'

'The suspect's DNA's on file,' Webb remarked.

'Then there should be enough to nail him.'

'Once we can catch him,' Webb qualified to Jackson, as they left the garage and walked down the road to the police station. They were shown to DCI Good's office.

'The blood they found is sure to match Judd's,' Good greeted them jubilantly, 'and with the other samples up our sleeve, I reckon we can clobber Baring as soon as we lay hands on him.'

'Just as well,' Webb observed, 'since he seems to be the only suspect. I've had the feedback on those names I mentioned, and they're all in the clear. Any sightings yet?'

'No, damn it, though every available man's out searching. Ten to one someone's hiding him.'

'Has his wife shown up?'

'No, nor likely to. She ran off with another bloke while he was inside—someone at Crossley's, where he works, told us. We've apprised them of the position now.'

'Has he contacted them?'

'Not since he scarpered.'

Webb frowned, drumming his fingers on the

desk. 'Had they any idea where he might go?'

Good shook his head. 'He's not particularly pally with anyone there.'

'Well, in this weather he could hole up outdoors without any problem.'

'Surrounding woods and barns are being scoured, and people asked to check their garden sheds, though we're warning them not to approach him. Railway and bus stations are on the lookout, also car-hire and taxi firms. Though if he nipped on a bus within minutes of legging it, he could be anywhere now.'

'It's only a question of time, Harry; we're bound to get him sooner rather than later.'

'I hope you're right. But he must know the media coverage the case is getting; stands to reason he'll be doing his damnedest to get away.' Good sighed. 'In the meantime, the Super's none too happy about the slip-up.'

'I can imagine. Well—' Webb rose to his feet— 'tomorrow's another day, but I've had enough of this one. I'm off home for a shower and a cold drink.'

'Good idea.' Good collected his papers together and slipped them into a drawer of his desk. 'As you say, we'll have to wait and see what tomorrow brings.'

*   *   *

'All right, old boy,' Frederick said, looking down at the dog sitting in front of him. 'I know what time it is. Go and get your lead.'

The retriever bounded out of the room and returned a minute later with it in his mouth. Frederick bent and fastened it to his collar.

Edwina said, 'Will you want coffee this evening, when it's so hot, or would you prefer a cold drink?'

'Coffee'll be fine, dear.' He bent to kiss her cheek. 'I'll be back in about twenty minutes.'

He said the same thing every evening, she thought fondly as he went out, the dog excitedly wagging its tail beside him.

Frederick stood for a moment on the doorstep, breathing in the rich perfume of nicotiana and night-scented stock which lined the front path. Across the green, the patrons of the Jester were standing outside on the pavement with glasses in their hands, laughing and talking. The floodlit church clock pointed to nine-thirty. Old Goldie must have a timing device—he knew exactly when his walk was due.

Just, Frederick thought, as he knew where to go, and would accept no deviation. He had set off, nose to the ground, pulling Frederick along behind him until they reached the corner, where he started down the road leading to the canal.

To be fair, the dog's conservatism was his own doing; he had been taking this same walk, with a succession of animals, every evening he'd been home for the last forty-odd years,

150

and at much the same time. During its course he had thrashed out many a theory on the criminal mind, reworked many a chapter ready for editing the next day. Occasionally, he would meet Jack Sharpe with his Airedale or John Smollett and Spot, but he seemed to remember both were on holiday at the moment.

It was a pleasant, residential avenue down which they were walking. Undrawn curtains offered a glimpse, should he want to take it, of his neighbours' sitting-rooms, most of them with the blue square of a television set glowing in one corner. Through open windows came the sound of radios, televisions, arguments, laughter. Life was lived much more publicly in the summer, he reflected.

They had reached the end of the road and open grass lay ahead of them, and the water, glinting in the moonlight. Just round the corner to their right was Hugh and Gillian's house. Occasionally, if he hadn't seen them for a while, Frederick would call in for a brief chat. Not this evening, though. He allowed himself to be dragged across the road to the canal bank, where Goldie waited to be released from his lead. Five minutes' free romp, then, at his whistle, the dog would return, docilely submit to being restrained again, and they'd begin the return journey.

The moon was full, sailing in a cloudless sky. Frederick lit a cigar, glancing across the silvered water at the harsher lights of cars streaming down the busy Broadminster road. Thank God his days of hurrying were over.

Contentedly he paced over the springy turf, keeping an eye on the antics of the dog gambolling ahead of him. The smoke from his cigar was pungent in the still air and the sound of the distant traffic, reaching him merely as a hum, only accentuated the silence. How lucky he was, to live in this lovely, peaceful spot.

The five minutes were up and Edwina would have the coffee on. He whistled for Goldie, refastened his lead and they crossed the road again to complete their circular tour up the next avenue along. Here, several large chestnuts lined the pavement, blotting out the moonlight.

Suddenly the dog halted, and to his surprise Frederick saw the fur rise along its back. What had startled him? As Frederick bent to reassure him, the dog growled low in its throat and in the same moment a shadow detached itself from the tree and Frederick was aware of a crashing, annihilating blow on his head before total blackness overwhelmed him.

* * *

The evening had brought little relief from the heat. Hugh and Gillian had taken their after-dinner coffee on to the terrace and were now sitting reading in the light from the room behind them, brushing away the occasional blundering moth.

Hugh checked the time. 'Do you want to watch *News at Ten*?'

'No, I saw it at six, and I've heard enough about that murder and Pop's theories on it to last me a lifetime.' She put her book down and stretched. 'Actually, I'm ready for bed. For the last ten minutes I've been trying to summon up the energy to go for a bath.'

She'd had a busy day, cleaning the house for tomorrow's visitors, shopping, and then preparing one or two of the courses for the dinner party. She wished uselessly that it was this time tomorrow, when it would be nearly over. Chiefly, she was worried that she might not be able to act naturally, knowing what she did. If only she'd not promised Roy to see Alex! Then she wouldn't know any more than anyone else—a much more comfortable state of affairs.

The phone cut into her musings and Hugh looked up in surprise. 'Who could be ringing at this time?' He got up and went through the patio doors.

'Hugh?' Edwina's voice sounded in his ear, taut with anxiety. 'Has Frederick called in to see you?'

'Frederick? No, why?'

At the sound of her father's name, Gillian came hurrying to Hugh's side and he held out the phone so they both could hear.

'He went out at nine-thirty as usual and he hasn't come back. You know how punctual he is—you could set your watch by him. He's always home by ten to ten.'

'Well, it's only five past,' Hugh pointed out reasonably.

'By his standards, that's late. I wonder—could you possibly go out and see if you can see him?'

'Well, yes, of course, if you know the way he went.'

'He always takes the same route. Down Sandford Road, five minutes on the canal bank, and home up Lismore Drive. I know it's silly, but I've had this nasty feeling all day. I wish now I hadn't let him go, but what excuse could I have given?'

'Don't worry, Edwina. I'll go and look straight away and phone you back, but by then I'm sure he'll be home.'

'Thank you,' she said distractedly, and hung up.

Hugh turned to his wife, meeting her wide eyes. 'Surely you're not worried as well?'

'Of course I'm worried! Mother's right, Pop's as punctual as Big Ben. If he's not back, something must have happened to him.'

'Gilly, he's a grown man, with a dog for protection, at that.'

'Goldie? He's just a big softie.'

'Well, I'll go and see what I can see.'

'I'm coming with you.'

'There's no—'

'I'm coming with you!' Her voice had started to rise, and he quickly touched her arm.

'All right, darling, all right.' He closed the patio doors, leaving their coffee cups outside on the table, and they hurried through the house and out of the front door. The garden was flooded with moonlight, a cold white clarity with sharply etched shadows beneath the hedge. At the gate they paused, looking left and right along the deserted canal bank opposite.

'Well, he's not there now,' Hugh said unnecessarily. Gillian ran to the corner of Sandford Road and looked anxiously up it. She could see only halfway, where the road curved to the left, but that stretch, too, was deserted.

'Shall I go up while you look in Lismore?' she asked Hugh, but he took hold of her arm.

'No way. I'm not going to lose you too— we'll stick together. Let's look at Lismore first, since he goes back that way.'

They heard the dog whining before they reached the next corner, and broke into a run, finding Frederick at once, a huddled heap on the pavement, with the dog distractedly licking his face and giving out that sharp, keening note. Hugh pushed it away as he knelt beside the prone figure. He saw with dread that the steel-grey hair was sticky with blood.

Gillian had given a cry and taken her

father's limp hand. 'Is he —? He's not —?'

'There's a faint pulse,' Hugh said, 'very faint. Go and phone for an ambulance, then ring your mother and tell her what's happened. And take the dog with you—leave him with Loveday. I'll stay here. Hurry, darling,' he added urgently.

She seemed paralysed with shock, but at his prompting stumbled to her feet, picked up the dog's lead and started to run home.

*   *   *

Gillian returned with Edwina before the ambulance arrived, having gone halfway to meet her mother. Hugh, meanwhile, without so much as a sweater to cover the still figure, had been massaging the flaccid hands between his, dreading the cessation of that fluttering pulse.

Edwina was icily calm. She knelt beside her husband and stroked his forehead, murmuring endearments, while the other two stood helplessly watching.

'Mother says they've had a break-in,' Gillian said through chattering teeth. 'She's only just discovered it; Pop's study has been ransacked, but nothing else seems to have been touched.'

The siren of the ambulance drowned Hugh's reply and they both turned thankfully, only too ready to release their charge to more experienced care. Once Frederick had been carefully lifted inside and Edwina'd climbed in

156

beside him, they hurried home to collect their car. It was going to be a long night.

* * *

Gillian felt she would never forget any detail of that hospital waiting-room, from the patterns on the curtains to the star-shaped burn in the carpet. Perhaps out of sympathy for anxious relatives, the nonsmoking rule seemed to have been waived, because there were ashtrays full of cigarette stubs, and stale smoke hung in the air.

Hugh had gone to phone Alex and Roy. Dully, Gillian wondered if this sudden crisis might bring them together. She turned to her mother, intending to say something rallying, but Edwina's set white face deterred her. She was clinging to her self-control, and any overt sympathy could threaten it. Frederick was undergoing tests and X-rays; they would be told the results as soon as possible, but when they last heard, he had not regained consciousness.

'I've been expecting something like this,' Edwina announced suddenly. 'Now that it's happened, in some ways I feel easier.'

Since there seemed no appropriate reply, Gillian said instead, 'We'll have to report the burglary.'

'I don't think anything valuable's been taken.'

157

'That's not the point, the—'

Edwina lifted a hand. 'I know, I know, but I have more important things on my mind at the moment. Tomorrow will be soon enough.'

'Do you think it's linked with the attack?'

'Wouldn't you say two assaults on your father in one evening is more than coincidence? It must have happened earlier, when we were watching TV. It was so hot I'd left all the windows open. No doubt that's how he got in.'

Gillian shuddered. 'He could have murdered you both.'

'I suppose he could, but he decided to settle for your father.'

Hugh returned with some coffee out of a machine.

'Alex is on her way; Roy's staying with the kids.' He handed them each a plastic mug. 'Not exactly the Ritz, but better than nothing.' He eyed Edwina cautiously. 'The police are outside, waiting to speak to Frederick.'

Gillian said on a half-sob, 'Then they are expecting—they do think he'll be—all right?'

Hugh put an arm round her. 'Of course he will. I told you he's a tough old bird.'

'I wonder if he got a look at his attacker,' Edwina mused, holding the mug between both hands as though she needed its warmth. 'If so, he'll still be in danger. Maybe that's why the police are here.'

Gillian said desperately, 'It *could* still be a

158

coincidence. Perhaps he was just mugged, a random attack that could have happened to anyone.'

'But he wasn't robbed,' her mother reminded her. 'Not during the attack, nor even, apparently, the break-in.'

'Since the police are here,' Hugh said gently, 'we might as well take the opportunity of reporting it. Shall I ask them to come in?'

Edwina hesitated, and Gillian saw with pity how close she was to breaking point. But she merely nodded, and Hugh went out to fetch them.

*   *   *

Harry Good phoned Webb with the news just after eleven-thirty, as he was preparing for bed.

'I was worried all along how Chummie would react when he heard about Mace. Silly old buffer just couldn't keep his mouth shut.'

'How is the old boy?'

'Hasn't come round yet. Must have a skull like concrete to have survived at all.'

'What are his chances?'

'There's a slight improvement, I'm told. But once word gets out that he's not dead—provided, that is, he does pull through—he'll need protection till this lot's cleared up. We've got a couple of blokes at the hospital, and one of them has just phoned to say the Mace house was broken into this evening.'

'Ye gods. What happened?'

'The old boy's study was ransacked, drawers pulled out, files emptied, etcetera, but as far as his wife could see, nothing's missing and none of the other rooms was touched.'

'You think it was Baring?'

'It has to be, hasn't it? God, if only he hadn't slipped through our fingers this morning!'

'At least it means he's still in the area.'

'Small consolation, but I suppose you're right.'

'Thanks for letting me know, Harry. I'll be over in the morning.'

'See you,' said Good, and hung up.

Webb replaced the phone and hesitated, wondering whether to ring Hannah. She'd be upset to hear of the attack. Better to let her get a good night's sleep and tell her in the morning. Sighing, he climbed into bed and switched off the light.

CHAPTER NINE

It was dawn before Frederick finally stirred and opened his eyes to find Edwina beside him.

She bent forward quickly. 'Darling, it's all right. You've had a nasty bang and you're in hospital.'

His face was as white as the bandages round his head, but she saw memory flicker in his eyes and he said urgently, 'The dog —?'

'He's fine. He didn't desert you; Hugh and Gilly found him licking your face and whining.'

'More to the point if he'd taken a mouthful out of the bastard that did *this*.'

Edwina's eyes filled with tears of relief. 'Now I *know* you're going to be all right!' she said.

*   *   *

By eight o'clock that morning, the police had sealed off Brighton Villa while SOCO subjected it to a detailed examination.

The point of entry was immediately established as the kitchen, where the sash window, left open a few inches, had been pushed up sufficiently to enable someone to climb through. That someone had worn rubber-soled shoes, though not, it appeared, the ubiquitous trainers—in what at first glance looked to be a size nine; and, of course, gloves. Still, shoe-prints could be as damning as finger marks these days.

Fortunately there was a flowerbed beneath the window, which had been assiduously watered by Edwina as soon as the sun was off it, and small clods of damp earth charted the intruder's progress down the hall, past the

161

room where the couple had presumably been sitting, to the study at the front of the house.

'Probably glanced through the open door on his way upstairs, and thought there might be a safe in there,' one of the SOCOs remarked.

'He was taking a risk,' another commented. 'Anyone passing the house could have looked up and seen him.'

'We don't know what time he broke in,' pointed out the DI in charge. 'If it was before about eight-thirty, the evening sun would have been shining on the windows, which would have screened him. And after that, the light would have been too indistinct. Anyway, judging by the fibres the tape's picking up, he knelt down while he searched the desk.'

He looked about him at the sheaves of papers, open books, and upturned drawers which littered the room. 'It's not surprising the old girl couldn't tell if anything's missing, and it'll be some time before her husband can check. Still'—he indicated the desk— 'Chummie didn't get it all his own way; the bottom drawer's still locked. From all those chips lying around, he had a good go at it, but he wouldn't have dared make too much noise, with both of them in the house.'

The mess that the intruder had left was as nothing to that made by the fingerprint men with their pervasive powder, which they sprinkled liberally on surfaces and papers alike. Smudged prints were in abundance, left by leather gloves—unbearably hot, surely, on such an evening. The index finger of the right hand appeared to have a little nick out of the leather—which would be useful, were they ever able to track it down.

The men gave up speculating and settled down to their thorough and painstaking task.

*   *   *

Hugh said, 'I think the dinner party should go ahead.'

Gillian looked at him in dismay. 'Sonia! I haven't rung to tell her what's happened.'

'So much the better; you've done most of the preparations, haven't you?'

'Yes, but what about Alex? She'll be as tired as we are; we didn't leave the hospital till gone two, and Roy would have waited up for her.'

Once Frederick had been taken off the critical list, Edwina had insisted that her daughters went home.

'Really, darling,' Hugh persisted, 'it's best to carry on as planned. You're going in to see your father this morning; there's no more you can do, and it will be therapeutic for you and Alex to have something else to think about. Ring her and see what she says.'

Quite apart from her tiredness, Alex would have been only too glad to cancel the evening, now she knew about Sonia's suspicions. On the other hand, Gilly had gone to a lot of trouble,

163

and it *would* take their minds off their father. And after all, the baby-sitter was booked.

'All right,' she said finally. 'If you can face up to having us, the least we can do is come. We'll be there at eight, as arranged.'

*   *   *

A tent had been erected over the scene of the attack and a uniformed constable left on guard overnight. Now, a group of SOCOs was engaged in the laborious business of photographing the area and taking samples from the pavement.

The to-ing and fro-ing the previous evening—by the family and the ambulance staff, not to mention the dog—had done much to obliterate any clues there might have been. The dried blood was almost certainly Mace's, which later tests verified, and the only other find was a few minute particles of soil matching the samples from inside the Mace house and originating from their garden.

The soles of Mace's own shoes had been clean, but the particles could as easily have been carried on the paws of the dog or the shoes of the family—still to be examined—as those of the attacker.

All in all, it was a disappointing result.

*   *   *

Hugh and Gillian had not allowed for the extent of Frederick's new-found celebrity. Reports of his attack were given on the news bulletins, and Sonia phoned just as Gillian was leaving for the hospital.

'Gilly, is it true? I couldn't believe it! How is he? How perfectly awful!'

Gillian gave her a concise account of what had happened, adding, 'We're still expecting you this evening.'

'Oh, but we couldn't put you to that trouble—not now!'

'Son, it's for Alex's and my sake as much as yours. Please come.'

'But I'd feel dreadful—you arranged it for me in the first place, and now that this has happened, I—'

'Please, Sonia. Look, I must go—I said I'd be at the hospital by eleven.'

'Well, as long as you're quite sure. And do give your father my love. As soon as he's fit for non-family visitors, I'll be in to see him.'

*   *   *

There were some non-family visitors, however, who had already called on Frederick. DCI Good and his sergeant had arrived at the hospital soon after ten.

'Mr Mace, I've been limited to five minutes

165

and I'll try not to tire you, but there are some questions I must ask.'

'Fire away,' Frederick said resignedly. He had one hell of a headache, his eyes were bloodshot, the skin surrounding them a luscious purple, and all he wanted to do was sleep. But it was only reasonable that he should grant the police their interview.

'Most importantly, did you get a look at your attacker?'

'Not a glimpse. It was dark under the trees, the dog suddenly stopped and growled, and as I bent to soothe him I was aware of a moving shadow. That's all.'

'Have you any idea what might have occasioned the attack?'

He shrugged. 'Unfortunately I've a fairly high profile at the moment. It's easy to make a remark which antagonizes someone, though luckily not many carry their objections this far.'

'You've not received any threats?'

'No.'

Good shifted on the less than comfortable chair. 'I don't know if your wife told you there was a break-in at your home last night?'

'Yes, she mentioned it. I gather nothing was taken.'

'As far as we know. Could you tell me, sir, what you keep in the bottom drawer of your desk?'

'Why?' The question shot out with all

Frederick's usual vigour. 'Did he get into it?'

'No; he tried, but without success.'

'Thank God for that. It contains the work on my latest book. As my family will tell you, I'm paranoid about whatever I'm working on, and always keep it under lock and key.'

'Who's likely to know that, sir?'

'Well, the family, of course, and possibly my research assistant, but I can't think of anyone else.'

'Might the intruder have been looking specifically for notes on your book?'

'It depends who he was, doesn't it, Chief Inspector?'

There was a brief pause, then Frederick said, 'Well, if that's all, may I ask you a question?'

'Of course, sir.'

'I presume the Feathers investigation is still open?'

The question took Good by surprise. 'Yes, it is, but as you'll appreciate—'

'Then I have an urgent message for the officer in charge. Will you make sure he gets it?' He caught Good's instinctive movement, betraying the impatience of the professional towards the meddling amateur, and went on drily, 'Oh, I'm sure you think I'm a blundering old fool who talks more than is good for him'—Good shot him a startled glance—'but this could be of vital importance, so please humour me.'

'Of course, sir,' the chief inspector said hastily. 'What's the message?'

'That it seems Trevor Philpott was consistently unfaithful to his wife. I believe that likelihood has not emerged before.'

'Well, no. Quite the contrary, in fact. May I ask—?'

'I went to see his widow. She didn't intentionally keep it from you—she herself found out only last summer, when she met some former friends. I did ask her to contact you, but I wanted to make doubly sure it got through, because if I'm not mistaken, it could provide the motive, you've been searching for. There's another thing, too, though this mightn't have any significance: it seems he was homophobic. There was an unpleasant scene one evening, when he insulted a couple of homosexuals.'

Good nodded. 'I'll make sure the message is passed on, sir.'

'Thank you.' Frederick lay back against his pillows, drained of what little energy he had. A nurse appeared at the foot of the bed, gave the policemen a severe look, and imperiously beckoned them out of the room. Meekly, they rose and followed her.

'Do you think that was on the level, Guv?' Sergeant Deakin inquired as they went down the broad, linoleumed stairs. 'About Philpott carrying on? First we've ever heard of it.'

'Search me, Stan, but the old boy seems to

168

think it's important. I'll give DCI Ferris a bell when we get back to the station.'

*   *   *

However, within minutes of their return to Albion Street, all thought of Frederick Mace had been pushed from their minds. Lee Baring had been sighted and had taken cover in a wood to the east of the town. The area was surrounded and it seemed the net had closed at last.

'Why the hell didn't you get me on my mobile?' Good exploded.

'It's only this minute come through, Guv. I was about to call you when I heard you'd arrived downstairs.'

'Get on to DCI Webb—pronto. He's the Investigating Officer.'

The message reached Webb as he and Jackson were on their way to Ashmartin, and Jackson diverted the car to make directly for the targeted area.

'Is he armed?' Webb asked Good.

'I'd say it's unlikely, since he wasn't planning to leg it. He simply scarpered when we flagged his car down.'

'Right. See you at the rendezvous in ten minutes.'

*   *   *

169

The senior detectives arrived on the scene simultaneously, in time to see Baring being led, handcuffed, out of the wood by two uniformed constables. The small crowd that had gathered gave an ironic cheer, and someone called, 'What's he done, then?'

He did not receive a reply.

Baring was a pathetic figure, white-faced and in need of a shave. So much for the ruthless, scheming double-murderer they'd been searching. As so often at this stage of an inquiry, Webb felt a sense of anticlimax. He watched while the man was bundled unceremoniously into a police car. Good, who had been speaking to one of the constables, came back to join him.

'He didn't say a dicky-bird when he was cautioned. We'll see what happens back at the station.'

Webb grunted and Good glanced at him reprovingly. 'You don't seem exactly elated, Dave. What's up?'

'I was looking at his feet,' Webb said.

'His feet?'

'If those shoes are size nine, I'm a Dutchman.'

*　　*　　*

Baring denied all knowledge of Simon Judd, which, Webb supposed glumly, was only to be expected. Seated next to the duty solicitor, he

170

also refused to give any explanation of his flight from the police officers, other than expressing a conviction that they were 'out to get' him.

When asked for what, Baring retorted darkly, 'Don't need a reason, do they? They collar you first, then think up something.' Which didn't exactly conform with PACE.

As agreed, Good was conducting the first part of the interview, but it was fast reaching an impasse by the time a DS tapped at the door and asked for a word with him. The DCI went outside, returning a minute later with a triumphant look on his face.

'You still maintain you've never met Simon Judd, Mr Baring?'

'I keep telling you, don't I?'

'You do indeed. But you'll be interested to hear some samples removed from your car prove beyond doubt that he's been in it.'

Baring frowned, glancing at his solicitor for elucidation—which, however, was not forthcoming. 'Samples?' he repeated aggressively. 'What samples? Think I'm a bleeding commercial traveller?'

'Traces of his blood and several hairs, together with fibres from the jacket he was wearing.'

Finally realizing the implications, Baring half rose to his feet, before being restrained by the solicitor's hand on his arm.

'That's a bloody lie! There's *nothing* in that

171

car—I scrubbed it out myself. You're—'

'Mr Baring!' interrupted the solicitor. 'I strongly advise you to say nothing further.'

'But listen to 'em—they're trying to fit me up!'

Webb, watching the man closely, sensed his uncertainty, his fear.

'Blood, hairs and fibres,' Good repeated deliberately, 'which definitely link Mr Judd to your car.'

'Hold on a minute' —Baring licked his lips nervously—'I've just thought—that'd be the night it went missing. Slipped my mind for a moment, like, but it must have been then, 'cause I was leaving next day on the trip and in a right state, I can tell you.'

Good treated him to a long disbelieving look, and the man blundered on. 'Parked outside as usual after work, and when I went out to the pub later, it'd gone.'

'You reported it, of course?'

'Nah. When have the police ever done me any favours? Ten to one *I'd* have ended up the villain, like you're making out now.'

'And it reappeared just as suddenly?'

'Eh?'

'Your car; it came back of its own accord?'

'Oh—yeah. Next morning when I looked out, there it was, large as life, a bit further down the road. Gawd, was I glad to see it!' He flicked a quick look at Good, and added, 'Kids, I expect.'

Good sighed. 'I'm sure you don't expect me to believe that.'

'Believe what the hell you like,' Baring said defiantly, 'it's the truth. And if you're on the level about them hairs, it would explain how they got there without me knowing.'

Webb leant forward, entering into the questioning as previously arranged. 'Where were you last evening, Mr Baring?'

The man looked at him uncertainly, unsure of this second approach. 'Last evening?'

'Between eight-thirty and ten pm.'

Baring glanced from him to Good and back again, sensing a trap. 'What's that got to do with this Judd bloke?'

'Just answer the question, please.'

'Well, I was keeping out of the way of you lot, wasn't I?'

'But where exactly? You were seen leaving the M4 motorway at ten-thirty yesterday morning, where you failed to comply with a request to stop. When you eventually did so, you evaded the officers and ran off into the Hazeldene housing estate. That was at approximately ten-forty-five. We would like to know how you spent the next twenty-four hours.'

'Lying low, like I said. I bought bread and cheese and cans of beer and made for the woods till things died down a bit.'

'If you're as innocent as you claim, why were you so anxious not to be caught?'

Baring snorted. 'I was innocent last time, and a fat lot of good it did me. Went down for three years, didn't I?'

Keeping his eyes steadily on the man in front of him, Webb said slowly and deliberately, 'I put it to you that sometime during yesterday evening you broke into a house belonging to Mr Frederick Mace, and ransacked his study.'

Baring was staring at him wide-eyed.

'And later,' Webb continued, with more assurance than he felt, 'you lay in wait for him when he walked his dog, jumped him and submitted him to a vicious attack.'

Baring found his voice at last, and shrilly. 'There you go again!' he cried. 'I don't know what the bleedin' hell you're on about—I never went near no house and I didn't attack no one, neither.'

'Just a minute, Chief Inspector,' the solicitor broke in. 'I wasn't given notice of this line of questioning. Are you now accusing my client of another crime, and if so, *how* does it tie in with the current inquiry?'

Webb said heavily, 'We believe it does tie in; *how* is what we're trying to establish.' He turned back to Baring. 'What size shoes do you wear, Mr Baring?'

Emboldened by his solicitor's intervention, Baring mimed incredulity. 'What is this, twenty bleeding questions?'

'Your shoe size, please?'

174

'Sevens, if it's any of your business.'

'Would you remove a shoe and hand it over?'

Baring glanced at the solicitor, who nodded impatiently. Webb took the proffered brogue—not, he noted, rubber-soled. It was indubitably a size seven, which came as no surprise. Therefore, as Webb had suspected when he first saw the man, whatever else Baring had done, he had not broken into the Mace house. So who the hell had, and why?

* * *

Patrick said, 'You're not saying the dinner party's still on?'

'Yes; I phoned Gilly as soon as I heard, and she was most insistent. I suppose it will help take her mind off things.'

'But ye gods, with her father at death's door, if not already dead? Surely—'

'He isn't, actually—he seems to be pulling through, thank God. I'm very fond of old Frederick; I've known him so long he's like a second father.'

Patrick rubbed a hand over his eyes. 'Well, I'm glad to hear it, of course, but when I heard the news, the prospect of an evening in was very welcome. I'm totally shattered. God,' he added after a moment, 'I didn't mean that the way it sounded.'

Sonia laid a hand on his arm. 'You do look

175

pale, darling; what's wrong?'

'Mother—what else? I nearly phoned you, but there was little point. She had another attack this afternoon.'

'Oh, Patrick, I'm so sorry. How is she now?'

'Very weak. It's no good, Sonia, she's too much for Zoë to manage any longer.'

Sonia felt a clutch of dread. 'So what will you do?'

'God knows. I suppose I'll have to find a home of some sort. She'll hate it, but there's no option.'

He turned abruptly and went to the drinks cabinet. 'Is there no way we can get out of this dinner?'

'Not really, in the circumstances. We owe it to Gilly and Alex to turn up.'

Patrick's hand stilled briefly. Alex. Sweet mercy, he could do without this. 'Can't you say I'm unwell?'

'Look, *you* need some light relief as much as they do. There's no more you can do this evening, so relax. You might even enjoy it.'

However, Sonia thought as she changed to go out, the original purpose of the evening was unlikely to be served; Gilly would be in no condition to assess Patrick's attitude, and in any event he was under par himself. The object now would be to offer moral support at a difficult time; any other consideration would have to be postponed.

Roy said anxiously, 'Are you sure you feel up to this?'

'I've told you I'm all right. Stop fussing.'

'You seem very much on edge to me.'

'Of *course* I'm on edge! How could I be anything else?'

'But he's out of danger, darling. You must try to calm down.'

Alex made a dismissive gesture. She could hardly explain it was the prospect of being with Patrick and Sonia which at the moment was uppermost in her thoughts.

She reached for the scent bottle, then stopped with her hand in midair as she remembered Gillian's warning: *For God's sake don't wear your Chanel.* Pulling open a drawer, she searched for an alternative, unearthing an old and almost empty bottle of Rive Gauche. That would do. She tipped it over her wrists, shaking out the last drops, then, glancing in the mirror to check her hair, saw Roy's reflected image, still anxiously watching her. She forced a smile and swivelled to face him.

'I'm sorry to be so grumpy; lack of sleep, probably.'

He smiled back, accepting the apology, though he knew, as she did, that her bad temper was of longer duration and had deeper roots.

The front doorbell chimed, heralding the

arrival of the baby-sitter. Alex stood up, smoothed down her skirt, and, with the unfamiliar scent of Rive Gauche in her nostrils, went down to let her in.

*   *   *

Her father's attack having pushed everything else from her mind, it was only when Sonia and Patrick arrived that Gillian recalled with a start the reason for the dinner—a reason which, in any case, no longer held. For what need had she to study Patrick's behaviour when she already knew Sonia's suspicions were well founded? She felt a stab of pity for her friend.

Her eyes went from Sonia's determinedly bright face to Patrick's pale one, wondering if they realized that their body language betrayed them. In some indefinable, and no doubt unconscious, way, Patrick was holding himself apart, separate from his wife even as she leaned slightly towards him. Gillian saw his eyes flick quickly to Alex, then away as sharply as if their exchanged glance had burned him.

Sonia came forward to kiss her. 'How are you, love?'

'Coping, and very glad to see you both. What would you like to drink?'

Gillian wondered if she sounded as stilted to the others as she did to herself. The evening was not boding well; Alex was jumpy, Roy

178

guarded, she and Hugh tired. Now Sonia and Patrick had brought their own anxieties to add to the already fraught atmosphere.

Quite suddenly, the prospect of walking on eggshells all evening seemed unbearable, and it was only by a conscious effort of will that she prevented herself from running upstairs and leaving them all to their own devices.

Then Hugh came into the room with a tray of glasses. As though he sensed her distress he looked quickly across at her, and in that held glance she read love, reassurance, encouragement. He would help her out; he always did. She gave him a shaky smile and turned back to her guests.

* * *

Some hours later, Gillian was sitting up in bed, an unread book propped in front of her, listening to the sound of the shower from the adjoining bathroom. Well, the evening was over, thank heaven, and all things considered, it had gone reasonably well. As far as she could tell, Sonia had no inkling that Alex was the other woman in Patrick's life; her attitude towards her was as natural and friendly as always.

And after a shaky start, Alex herself, drawing on some inner reserve of energy, had sparkled and bubbled as though she had no cares in the world. Gillian had seen Roy's eyes

179

on her, puzzled, but with a faintly dawning hope. Oh God, what a mess it all was! If only she could discuss it with Hugh; but she'd promised Alex to say nothing.

He reappeared in her line of vision through the half-open door, vigorously towelling himself dry.

Echoing her thoughts, as so often happened, he commented, 'Alex seemed in good form, for a change.'

'Yes, I was just thinking that.'

'Wonder what brought it on. Perhaps your pep talk the other day.'

'Perhaps,' Gillian said noncommittally.

'Patrick seemed a bit under the weather,' Hugh continued, in an unnerving, if unwitting, sequence of thought.

'His mother's had another attack—Sonia told me. It's a constant worry for them both.'

'And his sister's rather a broken reed, from what I remember.' Hugh came into the bedroom, the towel draped strategically round his waist.

'Son's terrified that if his mother goes into a home, he'll want Zoë to live with them.'

'I shouldn't envy her that.' Hugh shed his towel and climbed into bed beside her.

'I was very proud of you this evening, Mrs Coburn,' he commented, slipping an arm round her. 'You looked gorgeous, as always, and, despite the last twenty-four hours, carried everything off with aplomb—no mean feat.'

180

'I was glad of your support,' she answered, leaning against him. Then, suddenly, she sighed. 'Oh, Hugh, whatever would I do without you?'

'I'd rather you never found out!' he answered, and bent to kiss her.

CHAPTER TEN

Harry Good didn't know what time it was—the middle of the night, anyway, and he was damned if he could get to sleep. He longed to talk the case over with his wife—she'd a sound head on her shoulders, and he valued her opinion—but despite the tossings and turnings by which he'd surreptitiously hoped to waken her, she slept on, and he'd had to abandon the attempt.

With a sigh, he turned his pillow over yet again in search of a cool patch of linen, tucked it under his chin, and allowed his overactive brain to resume its treadmill.

That toerag Baring was still playing games with them; the story of the stolen car was so much baloney, though they'd no means of proving it. So what had they got? His car'd been seen at the crucial time entering the pub car park, and the blood, hairs and fibres proved conclusively that Judd had been in it at some stage.

But frustratingly enough, there was nothing other than ownership of the car to put Baring himself on the spot. The only witness to have come forward had caught a glimpse of the corpse, not of the driver. Which was a case of sod's law, if ever there was one.

And, as Baring's solicitor had not failed to point out, since they'd been unable to establish any link between his client and Judd, what possible motive could he have had for killing him? It was the Feathers case all over again.

As for the murder weapon, Baring's house and garden, together with the surroundings of the Nutmeg, had been exhaustively searched, to no avail. But hell's teeth, the bloke had left next day for a tour of the bloody country. He could have dumped it anywhere.

Good turned over restlessly. And as if all that wasn't enough, Dave Webb was convinced it wasn't Baring who'd attacked old Mace. Which meant they had *two*—

Mace! As the old man's face formed in his mind, he remembered the urgent request he'd promised to attend to—and instantly forgotten. Well, a day's delay wouldn't make much difference; ten to one there was nothing in the old boy's theories anyway.

Good eased into another position, considering the message he should have passed on.

Philpott had apparently been consistently unfaithful to his wife.

Which, if true, was certainly a turn-up for the book. The picture painted at the time had been of a blissfully happy marriage, roses round the door and all the rest of it. Amazing, if Mace was right, that the wife hadn't cottoned on he was two-timing her. Or had she exaggerated her husband's peccadilloes for Mace's benefit, knowing his interest in the case?

She'd met some old friends, he'd said. Well, there are always 'friends' who enjoy stirring things up. Perhaps after all it was nothing stronger than malicious gossip—which probably also went for his anti-gay stance. No doubt the same 'friends' had told her that, too.

In the dining-room below, the clock whirred preparatory to striking. Morosely, Good counted the chimes. Four. If he didn't get some sleep soon, he'd be good for nothing in the morning.

He heaved himself over yet again, pushing aside the duvet in search of air. He'd performed this manoeuvre twice already, only to pull it back again minutes later, feeling chilly. Who'd invented these damn-silly things, anyway? He wished Meg hadn't succumbed to their ubiquity and dispensed with the time-honoured sheets and blanket, which at least gave you some control over your body temperature.

Very gradually, almost without noticing, he drifted at last into sleep.

*　*　*

It was time, Webb told himself later that morning, that he met Frederick Mace. The old boy had been on the edge of the case from the very start; Webb had seen him on television, heard him quoted on all sides, listened to Hannah's account of his talk and read all the press reports of it. Now, in one night, Mace had got himself attacked and had his house broken into, and while Webb still didn't think it was connected with the Judd case, as officer in charge it behove him to investigate the incident.

He reached for the phone and dialled Harry Good's number. 'I'm thinking of calling on old man Mace. Where is he, exactly?'

'In the QE—Queen Elizabeth Hospital, on Denham Hill. If you're coming from—'

'It's OK, I know where it is; we passed it *en route* to Mrs Judd. Ward number?'

'He's in the private wing—a room to himself. There'll be a copper outside—you can't miss it. And Dave, would you give him a message for me? Tell him I've been on to Ted Ferris at Erlesborough.' No need to add it was only five minutes ago.

'Oh?'

'He asked me to tell him that it seems likely Philpott had had a string of lady friends.'

'Really? How did he dig that one up?'

184

'From the widow, no less, but I'm taking it with a pinch of salt.'

'OK, Harry, thanks. I'll be in touch later. Nothing new on Baring?'

'What do you think?' said Good disgustedly.

*   *   *

It was a close day, the sky pewter-grey with no hint of sunshine, but the heat was unrelenting. A bit of thunder might clear the air, Jackson thought, following the familiar road to Ashmartin.

'How do you think Mr Mace can help, Guv?' he asked curiously. 'He didn't see his attacker, did he?'

'No, but he might have some inkling who it could have been. Here's the turning now, Ken.'

They were directed to the first floor of the hospital, and from the stairhead, as Good had intimated, a uniformed figure could be seen outside a door halfway down the corridor. Between it and them was the nurses' station, where they identified themselves and were allowed to proceed.

Webb again presented his warrant card to the bobby on guard and the young man stood to attention.

'Has anyone tried to gain entry, Constable?' Webb inquired.

'No, sir.'

'You've been told to ask everyone for

identification?'

'Yes, sir.'

'Beware the men in white coats,' Webb added with heavy humour.

The PC looked puzzled. 'Sir?'

'Come now, surely you've seen all those films where the villain gets past the armed guard by the simple expedient of borrowing a white coat and posing as a doctor? I'm just saying, be extra vigilant with anyone in a white coat.'

'Yes, sir. Thank you, sir.'

Webb winked at Jackson, knocked on the door, and went inside.

Frederick Mace was sitting up in bed reading the *Daily Telegraph*, a cup of coffee on the table beside him.

'DCI Webb, sir, from Shillingham, and my colleague, Sergeant Jackson.'

'Good morning, gentlemen. Come in and sit down.'

Webb drew a chair up to the bed, while Jackson plonked himself against the wall and took out his notebook.

'I hope you're feeling a bit better?'

'Much, thank you, even though I do look like a Turner sunset.'

The area round his eyes was streaked with purple and yellow, the eyes themselves still bloodshot.

'You were very lucky, Mr Mace. That blow would have shattered most men's skulls.'

'Tough as old boots—always have been,' rejoined the old man, with obvious pride.

'You didn't see your attacker?'

'Not so much as a whisker.'

'Were you aware of *anything* that might identify him—a particular smell, perhaps—sweat, tobacco, aftershave?'

Frederick thought for a moment, then regretfully shook his head. 'I'm afraid not. It all happened so suddenly.'

'Have you any idea who might have had it in for you?'

Frederick surveyed him, raising one eyebrow. 'The odd murderer, perhaps? I have been, as the Americans say, shooting off my mouth rather a lot lately.'

Webb smiled. 'You've certainly been hitting the headlines. I gather you're convinced the murders aren't connected?'

'Oh, they're *connected*, Chief Inspector.' And, seeing Webb's surprise, he went on, 'That is to say, one was taken as a blueprint for the other. That must be so, surely. But I'm quite certain we have two different killers.'

He could be right, Webb reflected; at least it wasn't Baring who had broken into the house. Had it, then, been Philpott's killer, who, when he couldn't find what he wanted, went after the old man in the hope that any information he held was only in his head?

'Well, Mr Webb?' Frederick prompted as he remained silent. 'I expected you to disagree with me; are you, too, coming round to the idea of two murderers?'

'All we can do is go by the evidence. I'm aware of your theory, though, that a serial killer would go for the same type of victim each time.'

'And these two were very different, weren't they? I was positive from the first that Philpott was a ladies' man, despite all the protestations to the contrary. Well, now it looks as though I was right.'

'That reminds me,' Webb put in, 'DCI Good asked me to tell you he's been in touch with Erlesborough.'

'Excellent. Then things should start moving.'

'You think Philpott's involvement with someone precipitated his death?'

'I'm sure of it.'

'How did you learn about his— philandering?'

'From his widow, who is now Mrs Bradburn. Some old friends kindly told her when she bumped into them last summer.'

'Did she give you the name of these friends?'

'Not their surname. I rang back to ask, but she was out. Still, the police will follow it up, won't they? I suppose you're hoping Philpott identified his conquests?'

'It might be useful. Still, that's not really my problem; I wasn't involved in that case, but I *am* with Mr Judd, who was found on my patch.'

He glanced at the alert old face. 'I was particularly interested in a phrase you used the other evening—that he might have done his killer a "long-distance wrong". Could you enlarge on that?'

Mace shrugged. 'You know more about these things than I do, but in premeditated murder, surely it's unusual for the victim not to know his killer?'

'Yes, I grant you that.'

'It might be explained in Philpott's case by his being killed by a jealous husband, but I don't think that holds for Judd, who really does seem to have led a blameless existence. Yet *his* killer sounded more personally involved and was almost certainly fighting his own battles. Which, I must say, seems incomprehensible when Judd recognized neither his name, voice, nor appearance.'

Webb was prevented from commenting by a tap on the door, which opened to admit an elderly lady with short brown hair and a freckled face.

Seeing the two policemen, she came to a halt. 'Oh, I'm sorry. Am I interrupting?'

Webb and Jackson had risen to their feet. 'Not at all, ma'am,' Webb assured her. 'We were just leaving.'

'Chief Inspector Webb, my dear, and Sergeant—Jackson, is it? My wife.'

'I hope you've been telling him, Chief Inspector, that if he kept his nose out of your business, he wouldn't get it bloodied.'

The stern words were belied by the loving look she bestowed on her husband as she bent to kiss him.

Webb said diplomatically, 'If you're writing about true crime it's obviously safer to stick with old ones, but your husband has some interesting ideas.'

'Too interesting,' Edwina returned darkly. 'Look where they got him!'

'But if we can flush them out, my dear—and note, Chief Inspector, I said "them"—it will be worth the odd bump on the head.'

'Bump!' Edwina echoed indignantly. 'You were almost killed!'

She turned back to Webb. 'But since he wasn't, Chief Inspector, is the man likely to try again?'

'It's always a possibility, which is why we'd like to keep Mr Mace here for the time being, under police guard.'

'But good God, man,' Frederick objected, 'you might never catch him! I can't spend the rest of my life cooped up in this place!'

'I trust it won't be for too long, sir. In the meantime, if there's anything else you think of, or remember, the officer on the door can contact me at any time.'

'Let's hope we do clear it up quickly, Guv,' Jackson commented as they went back down the stairs. 'I shouldn't fancy trying to hold that one for long against his will!'

*　　*　　*

Sonia unwittingly passed the two detectives in the hospital car park. She was dreading the next half-hour, uncertain what state she would find her mother-in-law in and hoping no mention would be made of any long-term plans for either her or Zoë. The two of them had moved to the village of Honeyford, some ten miles from Ashmartin, after Zoë's breakdown, 'to be closer to Patrick'. It was Sonia's constant fear that Zoë might now wish to move closer still.

Outside the room she paused briefly to marshal her resources. Through the circle of glass in the door, she could see Zoë sitting beside her mother and holding her hand. Sybil, eyes closed, lay back against her pillows, looking, Sonia thought with quickened heartbeat, extremely frail.

She quietly pushed the door open. Zoë greeted her with a strained smile but the older woman didn't open her eyes.

'How is she?' Sonia asked softly, laying the flowers she had brought on the bedside cabinet.

'She had a reasonable night. They won't commit themselves much further.'

'Has Patrick been in?'

'Not yet.'

'He said he'd come as soon as he could, but he'd several appointments this morning.'

She pulled up a chair on the other side of the bed. The sick woman's shallow breathing barely lifted her chest. If Sybil wasn't aware of her presence, there was little point in staying, she thought uncharitably. Certainly her sister-in-law showed no desire for her company. Zoë's gaze had returned to her mother, and Sonia took the opportunity to study her, searching as she always did for resemblances to Patrick, and finding few.

Zoë was ten years younger than her brother, and would have been in her mid twenties when her illness struck. She'd not had much of a life, Sonia thought with pity; yet she was now such a negative personality that the thought of closer contact with her was unbearable. Which, Sonia upbraided herself, was a thoroughly selfish outlook.

Most importantly, how would Patrick react if she raised objections to Zoë living with them? Sonia admitted that she didn't know. She could no longer gauge Patrick's reactions to anything.

The woman on the bed stirred suddenly and opened her eyes. 'Sonia,' she said drowsily. 'How nice.'

Sonia leaned over and dutifully kissed her. 'How are you, Mother?' The word came unnaturally to her, but they all expected it.

'Tired, my dear. Very tired.'

'Would you rather I left?'

'Of course not,' Zoë protested, 'you've only just arrived! Look, dear, at these flowers Sonia brought. Aren't they lovely?'

'I meant,' Sybil explained faintly, 'that I'm tired of being a burden on everyone.'

'That's nonsense!' Sonia declared roundly, and broke off as she encountered Zoë's unreadable gaze. For while it was true Sybil hadn't been a burden to *her*—she'd not allowed her to be—she couldn't speak for the other two. Was that, despite their love for her, how Patrick and Zoë now regarded their mother?

'Of course it's nonsense,' Zoë was confirming, 'and you mustn't think it for a minute. We'll soon have you back on your feet.'

Sybil Knowles made a faint, protesting movement, but had not the strength to argue her point and there was an awkward silence. Then Zoë, taking her mother's closed eyes as indication that she'd withdrawn from the conversation, said unexpectedly, 'I heard about your friend's father. Patrick said you should have gone to supper there last night.'

'To Gilly's? Yes, we did.'

Zoë's eyes widened. 'You still went? But I thought he wasn't expected to live?'

'He's pulled through, I'm thankful to say, and Gilly was most anxious the dinner should

193

go ahead. In the circumstances it was quite a pleasant evening.'

Though Patrick remained as distant as ever, she thought despairingly, and when there'd be another chance for Gilly to observe him, goodness knew.

*   *   *

Hannah had carried a drinks tray out to the garden and put the wine bottle in its cooler under the trees. The garden was communal to all the flats, but though everyone contributed to its maintenance, few residents made use of it.

Hannah was an exception, and often strolled there when she returned from school, glad of its open spaces after the confinement of the classroom, and watching indulgently as her cat chased imaginary mice through the undergrowth or ran up the boles of the trees.

This evening, she was hoping that the informal start would ease any constraint the four of them might feel after Gwen's long absence. The initial meeting between them had gone well, and Gwen, who'd seemed a little tense on arrival, had visibly relaxed.

Hannah glanced over to where she stood chatting with Monica Latimer. The contrast between the two women was almost comical: Gwen was her usual untidy self, spraying hairpins in all directions as her French pleat rapidly came undone. Her indifference to clothes was manifest in the print dress which hung awkwardly on her gawky frame, and she'd slung a knobbly, home-knitted cardigan round her shoulders.

Monica, on the other hand, was as always not only beautifully dressed but groomed to perfection, this evening in apricot linen which set off her fair, greying hair. But then she'd every incentive to dress well; born Monica Tovey, since her father's death she had run the prestigious fashion store Randall Tovey with formidable efficiency tempered by a natural charm. In her hands it had risen to new heights and become known both nationally and internationally, a fame undreamt of by her grandfather, who had founded it.

'A penny for them,' Dilys said, holding out her glass to be refilled.

Hannah smiled. 'I was thinking how different we all are,' she admitted.

Dilys followed the direction of her glance. 'Dear Gwen,' she said, 'she's not changed that much, after all.'

*   *   *

The meal, served in Hannah's pretty dining-room, had gone well, and now the four of them sat over coffee, the room lit only by the flickering candles on the table. The window was open to the darkening garden, and the

195

night calls of birds reached them clearly.

'This is where Gwen says something like, "East, west, home's best!"' Dilys commented.

Gwen smiled and ducked her head.

'You are glad to be back, aren't you?' Dilys persisted.

'Yes—yes, of course.'

'But—?' prompted Monica.

'Oh, I don't know. I was away for nearly a year, after all. Time to get into a completely different way of things. I'm having to ease myself back.'

'You really liked it out there, didn't you, Gwen?' Hannah said quietly, topping up her coffee cup.

'Yes; and the strange thing is, in Canada I seemed to fit in immediately. It's now I'm home again that the adjusting has to start.'

'Would you like to go back?'

Gwen didn't reply at once. Her eyes were on the silver spoon as she stirred her coffee, and the rest of them sat in silence, watching her and waiting. Then she seemed to reach a decision and looked up.

'I hadn't meant to say anything, but you three are my closest friends. I know I can count on you treating this as confidential.'

They all nodded solemnly, and Hannah felt a twinge of unease, wondering what was coming.

'The fact is that I was offered a post out there.'

196

Her words, totally unexpected, dropped into the quiet room with the impact of a thunderbolt. Dilys and Monica instinctively turned to Hannah who, after all, would be the one most affected.

Gwen met her eyes. 'Forgive me—I shouldn't have said anything. I should have spoken to you first.'

Hannah moistened her lips. 'You mean you're seriously considering it?'

'Considering it, yes, but I haven't reached any decision. I want to get the new term under way and see if my feelings for Canada abate a bit.'

'Is this position at the school where you were?' Monica asked.

'Yes, the present head is leaving in a year's time. Of course, it's a challenge. It's a much larger school than Ashbourne, and I really don't know whether I could do it. Or whether I want to,' she added as an afterthought. 'After all, there's Mother to consider.'

Hannah was aware of mixed feelings. Only a couple of days ago she'd been resenting handing back the reins to Gwen. Now there was a possibility of retaining them permanently. *Would* she be offered the post if Gwen decided to go? It would depend on the Board of Governors. The post would be advertised; suppose they chose someone else over her? Could she bear to stay on? Also, she was fond of Gwen, and would miss her if she

197

left permanently.

Gwen said softly, 'You sensed I was holding something back, didn't you, Hannah?'

'I did wonder,' Hannah admitted.

'Would you take on Ashbourne if you were offered it?'

Hannah gave a little laugh and spread her hands. 'Not so fast! You spring this on me, then expect an immediate statement of intent. There are any number of things to consider.'

'Well, your ability isn't one of them,' Gwen said flatly. 'You could do it standing on your head.'

There was a short, uncomfortable pause. Then Dilys said, 'It's almost ten o'clock; do you think we could watch the news? I want to see if there's anything new on the local murder; since hearing Mace's talk I've been following it, and the attack on him makes it look as though he's on to something. Thank God he wasn't more seriously hurt.'

They went through to the sitting-room and Hannah switched on the set. After the national headlines came the announcement that a man was being held in connection with Judd's murder, and the scene switched to outside Ashmartin Police Station, where the crime reporter awaited his cue.

'The arrest of the man, who has not been named, came after the attack on criminologist and writer Frederick Mace, but as yet the police have not made any statement linking

198

him with it. Meanwhile, speculation is still continuing that the Judd case might be connected with the death of Trevor Philpott six years ago.' Photographs of the two victims appeared to one side of the screen. 'The bodies of both men were found in public-house car parks, some thirty miles apart. This is Steve Potter in Ashmartin returning you to the studio.'

'I knew Trevor Philpott,' Monica remarked, and the other three turned to her, all exclaiming at once.

'You never told me!'

'What was he like?'

'How did you meet him?'

She shook her head laughingly. 'Don't get excited, I don't mean socially, but he came into the store quite regularly.'

'With his wife, you mean?' Randall Tovey didn't cater for men.

'No, to buy presents. Underwear, jewellery, the occasional handbag or silk scarf.'

'No wonder it was such a happy marriage!'

Monica said consideringly, 'Actually, we didn't quite believe those reports. For one thing, the underwear he bought was in several different sizes!'

'Did you tell the police,' Dilys demanded, 'after he was killed?'

'No, of course I didn't. His poor wife was going through enough without that. Anyway, the garments could have been for his sisters.'

'But Monica'—Hannah leant forward urgently—'the police were looking for motives and couldn't find any. The story was that Philpott hadn't an enemy in the world, but if he was involved with other women, that would open up a whole new perspective.'

Monica looked troubled. 'I never thought of that, and after all, it was flimsy evidence at best.'

'Nevertheless, if I were you, I'd get on to them in the morning. It's not too late, the case is still open.'

'Just think,' Dilys said, wide-eyed, 'you might have been holding vital evidence!'

'Or *with*holding it,' Hannah added sternly.

'Goodness, you're making me feel like a criminal myself. All right, if you think I should, I'll phone the police in the morning.'

And I, thought Hannah, will phone one of them tonight.

*   *   *

In the flat on the floor above, Webb had set up his easel. Baring had been charged with evading arrest, but they couldn't hold him much longer without something considerably more substantial. Yet damn it, if he did kill Simon Judd, and the odds were that he had, there must be *something* that would incriminate him.

Webb began to sketch the man as he had

200

seen him across the table—close-set eyes, ragged haircut, in need of a shave. Given that, as old Mace postulated, Baring had never met Judd, why had he killed him? The all-important motive factor still eluded them.

Webb held his thoughts determinedly at bay as he sketched, aware that in the past his unconscious had picked up clues he had not registered until they came out in his drawings. Concentrate, then, on Baring's character and see what comes through. The expression on the pencilled face became clearer as he drew—surly, aggrieved, self-righteous.

So what had struck him most about the man? Bitter resentment, Webb thought, feeling his way; that's what had really come through, together with a conviction that he'd been wrongly accused and falsely imprisoned.

Though a familiar ploy when first arrested, by the time a man had served his time, such claims had usually been discarded. Not in Baring's case: he had nurtured his sense of grievance throughout his prison term, and three years later it was as strong as ever.

So who did he hold to blame? The police? Someone who had fingered him? The judge at his trial? The jury who'd found him guilty?

Hang on a minute! Webb felt a quickening of interest. What was it old Mace had said? 'A long-distance wrong'? *Suppose Simon Judd had been on that jury?*

He sat back, staring at the bleak face he'd

depicted. Suppose Baring really had been innocent, and that Judd had somehow been involved in convicting him? It would fit Mace's 'long-distance wrong' theory. On the other hand, he presumably wasn't hunting down the remaining eleven jurors—why had he picked on Judd?

Webb pushed back his stool and went to pour himself a drink, turning the possibility over in his mind. If that *had* been the case, Judd was unlikely to have recognized Baring's voice after so long, if, indeed, he'd ever heard him say more than a few words. The name he probably would have known, but that given on the phone was Jim Fairlie. What about the man's appearance? It was over three years since Judd had seen him, and probably never close at hand. He might have looked vaguely familiar, but no more than that.

Yes, Webb thought, excitement moving in him, it fitted. In the morning he'd get on to the Chief Clerk at Court and get him to look up Baring's trial, see if Judd had been on the jury. It was a long shot, but it had potential.

The phone rang and he lifted it, his mind still pursuing this new avenue.

'David?' Hannah's voice.

'Hello there.'

'I've just had Les Girls to supper.' That was Webb's name for them. 'Monica says Trevor Philpott was always in and out of the store, buying jewellery and underwear. *In different sizes!* Could that be important?'

'It could be a back-up, certainly.'

'Back-up?' She sounded disappointed.

'Your friend Mace again; he's heard that Philpott probably had a number of affairs.'

Hannah said a trifle tartly, 'I'm beginning to wonder what you'd do without Frederick Mace.'

'Actually, we're not managing so badly under our own steam,' Webb returned, his eyes on the face propped on the easel.

'I'm glad to hear it. Anyway, I persuaded Monica to phone the police in the morning.'

'Well done. At least it would be corroborative evidence, which we're somewhat short of. Why didn't she report it at the time?'

'Thought his wife had enough trouble and didn't like to speak ill of the dead. It never occurred to her it might provide a motive.'

No doubt others had kept quiet for the same reason, Webb thought resignedly, which was why the murderer had had a clear field for so long.

'Thanks for letting me know,' he said. 'I presume your guests have gone?'

'Yes.' She hesitated, tempted to tell him of Gwen's Canadian offer, but bound by her promise of silence.

'Sleep well, then,' he said.

'And you.'

Feeling suddenly rather flat, Hannah hung up the phone and began to prepare for bed.

CHAPTER ELEVEN

By ten o'clock the next morning, Webb had ascertained that not only was Judd on the jury which convicted Baring, but he had been its foreman.

'So much for Chummie denying all knowledge of him,' he said with satisfaction.

'You still have to place him at the scene, though,' Crombie reminded him.

'He won't hold out much longer. Something's bound to come up.'

And it did, by means of a phone call from Good.

'We've got him, Dave!' he crowed exultantly. 'Nailed him fair and square! Forensic have come up with one of his hairs on Judd's jacket. He can't wriggle out of this one.'

'Excellent!' Webb exclaimed. 'Just what we need. And I've some good news, too; I've come up with a motive.'

He outlined what he had discovered, and Good was jubilant. 'Well done, Dave. So the old boy was right on that one. Wonder if he'll point us to Philpott's killer?'

'He's already given us some ammo. Have you heard any more from Ted Ferris?'

'No, but he said he'd get straight on to it. How soon can you get over here? We can only hold Baring another couple of hours without charging him.'

'I'll be with you in thirty minutes,' Webb said.

He stood up, sweeping his papers back into a file.

'Progress?' Crombie inquired, looking up from his desk.

'Let's hope so; one of Baring's hairs has been found on Judd's jacket. Trouble is, if he sticks to his stolen car story, he could argue Judd must have picked up the hair from the passenger seat, which wouldn't get us much further. Still, we'll face that if and when it comes.'

*   *   *

Paul Blake put his head round the door and Frederick laid down his newspaper with a smile.

'My dear chap, good of you to come.'

Blake handed him a box of the hard-centred plain chocolates which were the old man's favourites. 'I've been keeping in touch with your wife, but I didn't want to intrude too soon.'

'She said you'd rung. I'm glad to see you, Paul. For one thing, I've been worrying about you.'

Worrying?

'I mentioned you, you see, in the course of my talk. Oh, not by name, but that I had a

205

researcher. Anyone really interested could make inquiries. Since our friend can't get at me now, he might have a go at you.'

'I'll watch my back, never fear. You've heard they're holding someone for Judd's murder?'

'I've just been reading about it. It'll be interesting to see if my theory's vindicated.'

'Too bad they can't charge him with the Feathers case, while they're at it.'

Frederick shook his head, then winced slightly. 'He's not guilty of that one, Paul— believe me. But the race is on now. Will we find Philpott's killer first, or will the police?'

Blake looked at him despairingly. 'Aren't you satisfied with one knock on the head?'

'That's why they're hanging on to me, damn it. I'm quite well enough to go home, but they won't hear of it. Which is why I'm concerned about you.'

'I'm anonymous enough; no one's seen *me* on TV or giving talks in public.'

'You think my attacker could have been at the library?' Frederick sounded startled.

'Not necessarily; you were fully reported in the press.'

'But if he was, and he was still here the next evening for the break-in and to bash me over the head, it points to his being a local man— Judd's killer rather than Philpott's.'

'It's hardly a Sabbath day's journey from here to Oxbury,' Paul pointed out.

'True.' Frederick brightened. 'Lucky,

anyway, that my notes were under lock and key, though to be honest they wouldn't have been much help to him. So far, we've only scratched the surface, but now that I'm feeling so much better, I intend to occupy my time more productively.

'Which reminds me: I've rung home a couple of times to ask Edwina to bring in my notebooks when she comes, but there's no reply and the answerphone's not on. Could you possibly pop round and, if no one's in, drop a note to that effect through the letterbox?'

'Of course.'

Frederick shot the younger man a look under his eyebrows. 'After which, I presume you'll be on your way back to Oxbury?'

'No, actually, I thought I'd avoid it for a while. Things will be hotting up once news of Philpott's reputed affairs breaks, and I don't want to tread on police toes.'

'But now's just the time to go, man, while we have the advantage! People speak freely in a bar, but they button up when the boys in blue arrive.'

To Frederick's surprise, Paul didn't meet his eyes. 'I'm sorry, sir, but I've rather a lot on at the moment. I'll see if I can fit it in next week.'

Frederick was considerably taken aback; this was the first time Paul had failed to fall in with one of his suggestions, and he found he did not appreciate it.

'By next week,' he said stiffly, 'any advantage we might have will have been lost.'

'I'm sorry,' Paul said baldly.

'Very well; I realize you have other things to do. I mustn't keep you.'

And Blake, rightly taking it as a dismissal, had gone, leaving the uncomfortable atmosphere behind him.

Damn! Frederick thought impotently. Damn, damn, damn! What had caused that sudden digging-in of heels? Had Frederick been taking him too much for granted? After all, as he'd just allowed, the man had other jobs besides working for him—a fact he tended to forget.

But he'd had the distinct impression it was that particular request Paul had balked at, that for some reason he was reluctant to go back to Oxbury. In God's name, why?

If only he weren't so dependent on others! Frederick fumed in an excess of frustration. If only he could get out of this place and see to things himself, he was sure he could come up with something.

There was a tap on the door and the uniformed constable looked in apologetically.

'Excuse me, sir, did that gentleman by any chance bring you anything?'

Frederick gazed at him blankly.

'Any fruit or —?' His eyes fell on the box of chocolates on the bed. 'Ah! I'm afraid I'll have to remove those, sir.'

'*Remove* them?' Frederick spluttered.

'Sorry, sir; I should have stopped him at the door, but he didn't appear to be carrying anything. Thought I'd better check, though, and it's as well I did, or they'd have had my guts for garters. I've got instructions, see, to confiscate anything edible that's brought in, for examination.'

And, bearing the offending box of chocolates, he left the room, leaving Frederick staring speechlessly after him.

*   *   *

Back in the interview room at Ashmartin, Webb studied the man across the table, comparing him in the flesh with his pencilled likeness. The resentment and antagonism were still there, but they were now overlaid by anxiety. Possibly Baring had detected a new confidence in the police officers.

The usual rigmarole was enacted, the tape switched on and Baring tensed, watching them closely.

'Now, Mr Baring,' Good began, 'since we last spoke we've obtained some important new evidence.' He paused, and the man moved uncomfortably on his chair. The solicitor beside him remained motionless. Webb was aware of his annoyance; Baring had been all but due for release.

The hair was produced in a plastic envelope

and Baring regarded it stonily. When no one spoke, he said defiantly, 'Another of them samples, is it?'

'Yes, and this one belongs to you. Furthermore, it was found inside the jacket belonging to Simon Judd. *Inside*, mind you. Speaks for itself, doesn't it? Couldn't have been picked up casually; it must have been when you were lugging him out of the car.'

Which disposed of that loophole, Webb thought with relief.

Baring stared at the small envelope which could condemn him. 'Who says it's mine?'

'It has your DNA.'

'But why should I kill a bloke I'd never seen in my life?' It was said with bluster, playing the only card left to him, and Webb wasted no time in disposing of it.

'But, Mr Baring, you *had* seen him, hadn't you? Every day of your trial, in fact.'

Baring stared at him, and Webb saw the sudden hopelessness in his eyes.

The solicitor frowned; obviously, this was news to him. 'Chief Inspector, I'd like a word with my client.'

But quite suddenly, Baring had had enough. Either he couldn't face his brief's recriminations, or he simply realized the game was up. At any rate, he burst out impatiently, 'Well, your client doesn't want a word with *you*!'

Good leant forward and offered him a

cigarette, moving the interview into a new phase. Baring took it, bent to the lighted match, then raised his head, inhaling deeply with half-closed eyes. Webb, the nonsmoker, nevertheless welcomed the ritual as a prelude to confession.

Good, who had also lit up, leaned back in his chair. 'Suppose you tell us about it,' he said. 'Remember you're still under caution.'

Baring inhaled again. 'First off, let's get one thing straight—I never done that robbery I went down for. Gawdsake, I'd no previous on violence, they should have known that's not my form.'

The fact that he was now suspected of something much more serious seemed, in his indignation, to have escaped him.

'I ask you,' he went on, warming to his grievance, 'how would you feel, knowing you're clean, being banged up while the real villains scarper? Circumstantial evidence— that's what they got me on. Bloke that ID'd me got it wrong—it happens.' He grimaced, tapping ash on to the saucer on the table. 'I'm not saying he done it on purpose, but he makes a cock-up, and I go down—his word against mine. Call that ruddy justice?'

No one answered and after a moment he went on: 'Gawd knows that was bad enough, but then the wife ups and legs it. One for the bright lights was Shirl, and I'm no use to her, cooped up inside, now am I? Really got to me, that did. Thought the world of her.'

He paused again, remembering his wife. Then, suddenly, he slammed his hand on the table, making all three men jump.

'And it was all that poncey sod's fault!' he burst out. 'Sitting there passing judgement, all prissy and mealy-mouthed, fair revelling in it, he was! The rest of 'em was on my side—I could feel it. Nice, ordinary folk, the lot of them. I'd have got off if it hadn't been for that bastard Judd. I caught his eye once, before he'd time to look away. Cold as a fish.'

Webb said almost gently, 'You can't know Mr Judd swung the verdict.'

'Oh yes, I bloody can! You should have seen the smirk on his face when he gave it. The rest of 'em wouldn't meet my eye. Ashamed, most likely. It was his fault all right, and I swore there and then he'd pay for it.'

'So what did you do?' prompted Good.

As so often happened, Baring was now actually enjoying himself, boasting of how he'd achieved his end. 'Well, see, I remembered that murder down Oxbury way a few years back, the one the bloke got away with. So I asked Shirl to bring in everything she could find on it. (This was in the early days, like, before she went.) I reckoned if I could knock off Judd and leave him in a pub car park, you lot would think it was the same bloke. And since you didn't get him last time,' he added logically, 'then you wouldn't get me, neither.'

'Wasn't it rather risky, taking a dead body to a busy car park? Any number of people could have seen you.'

Baring looked surprised. 'They'd not seen the other bloke. Anyway, it was getting dark by the time I got there, I made sure of that. Did meet one car as we turned in, which threw me a bit. Still, no harm done. I kept my cool and drove to the far end, pulled him out, dumped him between two cars, and drove off like a bat out of hell.'

'As it happens, Mr Baring, some harm, as you put it, was done. The driver of that car gave us a description of yours. A local garage remembered doing an MOT on it and supplied the registration number, and Swansea did the rest.'

Baring stared at Good disbelievingly. 'You're telling me I'm sitting here now because of that bloke in the gateway?'

'He gave us the first lead,' Good confirmed.

'Where and how did you kill Judd?' Webb asked.

'In the car.' Baring answered almost absent-mindedly, still numbed by the consequences of that chance encounter. 'Dropped something on the floor, asked him to pick it up, and clobbered him with the wrench. Nothing to it.'

'Presumably you were parked at the time.'

'Yeah, I'd driven him into the country. Piece of luck him turning out a social worker. I just spun him a hard-luck story, and he never

213

smelled a rat till right at the end.'

'What did you do with the murder weapon?'

Baring grinned mirthlessly. 'You'll have a job finding that, mate. Hurled it into a Welsh lake, didn't I, on me travels. And don't ask me which, neither, because they all look alike to me and I can't say their names anyway.'

Webb remarked, though without hope, 'You say you based the killing on the Feathers murder. Weren't you in fact responsible for that one, too? You might just as well admit it; you're going inside for a long while anyway, so it won't make much difference.'

Baring looked at him scornfully. 'Come off it. Wouldn't have tried to throw suspicion on meself, now would I?'

To which, Webb supposed, there was no answer. It would have been too easy, anyway. After all, there was still the man with the size-nine shoes out there somewhere.

* * *

It was Saturday afternoon, and Roy had taken the boys to a cricket match. As usual, they'd invited her to go with them, but of course they'd known she wouldn't. If she had to be bored, Alex told them, she preferred to be bored at home in comfort.

Restlessly, she prowled barefoot round the house. The cleaner had been the previous day, and there was nothing for her to do. She'd

214

prepared the supper, she'd finished her library book, and there was only cricket on television.

The house was dim and cool behind slanted blinds but outside the sun was merciless, killing stillborn any thought of doing some gardening. She was hot, sticky and depressed; there were all at once so many things to worry about—the hostility her father'd aroused, her marriage, her relationship with Patrick.

She stood in the middle of the hall, absorbing the atmosphere of the house. To her left the sitting-room clock ticked comfortably. Behind her in the kitchen the fridge gave one of its periodic roars and clicks. Outside, some boys shouted as they rode past on their bicycles.

It was no use ringing Gilly, she and Hugh would be at the club watching Loveday play tennis. Mother was probably at the hospital, but she didn't feel like making the effort of changing and driving there. She'd go along for a while this evening while Roy stayed with the twins, thereby avoiding having to spend the evening together and make small talk.

With both hands she lifted the heavy mass of her hair so the air could get to her neck. She'd tie it up—that would make her cooler. In fact, she decided, halfway up the stairs, she'd have a shower and wash it, let it dry naturally, and then pin it up. After which, to complete the cooling process, she'd make some fresh lemonade, using Mother's recipe.

It would help to fill in the time, and the boys would be glad of it when they got back.

In the bedroom she stripped, stepped out of her clothes and, leaving them in a damp little pile, walked naked to the bathroom, welcoming the breeze of her movement on her body. She would treat herself to the expensive shower gel she kept for special occasions.

Moments later she was standing under the cool water, lifting her head to let it run in prickly streams over her face and neck and dripping hair. She squeezed the gel into her palm and massaged her body, feeling the heat and stickiness drain away. Then, reaching for the shampoo, she turned her attention to her hair. It felt almost decadent, to be performing these rites at three o'clock in the afternoon.

It was as she was rubbing her hair dry that she thought she heard the doorbell. Who could it be? Perhaps Susie about the scout picnic? She'd said she'd be in touch, but anyone would be welcome, to help pass this interminable afternoon.

She shook back her damp hair, reached for the robe hanging on the door, and ran barefoot down the stairs, pausing to look through the spy-glass in the door. Patrick stood on the step outside.

Alex flung open the door, noticing in that first moment that he looked tired, and a muscle was jumping at the corner of his eye.

'Alex,' he said.

Suddenly aware of her appearance, she took him by the arm, pulled him into the house and shut the door. In the cool, dim hall they stood looking at each other.

He said, 'You smell delicious.'

'Patrick, what are you *doing* here? You know we agreed—'

'I was desperate to see you, and I remembered Roy talking about taking the twins to the match. Anyway, I had to get away for a while—everything's so—bloody.'

He reached for her, burying his face in her damp hair, and she held him tightly, trying to find words to comfort him. How selfish she was, thinking only of her own problems, while Patrick's mother was dying and his sister a constant worry.

'Sonia didn't suspect anything, the other night?' she asked, as the panic thought struck her.

'What? Oh—no, I don't think so.' He drew back a little, looking into her face. 'I should have asked after your father. How is he?'

'Bouncing back, as usual.'

'That's great; when's he coming home?'

'They're keeping him in for a while, for his own safety. How about your mother?'

'Not bouncing anywhere, I'm afraid. Nor likely to.'

She looked up at him, her eyes full of sympathy, and saw him change. Sympathy was no longer enough. He said hoarsely, 'Alex,' and slipped the robe from her shoulders. As his mouth caressed her throat she felt her need rising to meet his and the heavy weakness over which she had no control flowed over her. She half turned towards the sitting-room, but he caught her hand and pulled her to the stairs. 'Oh no, my love, I'm not making do with the hearth rug. Not when there's a bed ready and waiting.'

Their coming together was as frenzied as always. There was none of the tenderness she'd shared with Roy, Alex thought, as Patrick finally fell back against the pillows. And—oh God, he was in Roy's bed!

Suddenly and totally, shame engulfed her. She could ignore her conscience as long as their lovemaking was clandestine and exciting—in the car, under the hedgerows like gypsies, even, once, in a hotel. But here, in the bedroom she shared with her husband, it had suddenly shed its glamour and stood exposed for what it was—underhand, sordid, both of them deceiving those who loved them.

She turned away from him, helpless against a rush of tears.

'Hey!' Patrick was leaning over her. 'Sweetheart, what is it? Is there something you're not telling me?'

She shook her head. How *could* she tell him? She was as much to blame as he was.

'Alex!' He gently shook her shoulder. 'For God's sake tell me what's wrong.'

218

'Reaction, I suppose,' she said between gasps. 'It's been pretty bloody here, too.'

'My poor love.' He pulled her back into his arms, cradling her against him, and she lay passive, waiting for her laboured breathing to quieten.

She said with an attempt at a smile, 'I had a shower to cool me down. Now I need another.'

'Let's have one together.'

'No.' She struggled away from him. 'Look, you'd better go. I'll have to straighten things up in here, and I'm not sure what time they'll be back.'

'Surely there's no hurry.' He frowned, looking down at her. 'There *is* something; what is it?'

She said unwillingly, 'We should have settled for the hearth rug.'

'Ah, the marital bed has been sullied, is that it? Bit late to develop a conscience, love. Anyway, I'm a firm believer that what the eye doesn't see, the heart won't grieve over.'

She forced a smile. 'No doubt you're right.'

To her relief, he got up and began to dress and, slipping on the robe again, she went down to the door with him.

'I parked round the corner,' he said. 'Your reputation is safe.'

'As long as no one sees you leave.'

'They won't.'

She opened the door cautiously. Outside, the hot street was deserted. He gave her a

219

swift kiss.

'I'll be in touch. And don't worry, sweetheart, we're not hurting anybody.'

Glib words, she thought as she closed the door. She was no longer sure that she believed them.

CHAPTER TWELVE

By the end of Saturday afternoon, Lee Baring had been formally charged with the murder of Simon Judd. Not a bad day's work, Webb reflected, and now that the case was under wraps, he could take the couple of days' leave due to him. Counting Sunday, that would make three days in all; if Hannah was free, they might even go away somewhere.

He was whistling as he pushed through the swing doors of the police station on to the baking pavement. Before going home, he'd call at the hospital and give Mace the news. It would cheer the old boy up.

But when he got there, it was to find someone already with Mace, a tall, thin young man who rose uncertainly to his feet as Webb, after a quick tap, appeared in the doorway.

'Chief Inspector!' Mace greeted him. 'Come in, come in. I don't believe you've met my research assistant, Paul Blake. Chief Inspector Webb, Paul, in charge of the Judd case.'

Webb looked from one to the other. Despite Mace's heartiness, there was an air of constraint in the room. It seemed he had interrupted something. Blandly he took the bony hand the young man extended.

'I've come to tell you, Mr Mace, that Baring has just been charged with Simon Judd's murder. It'll be on this evening's news, but I wanted you to know first.'

'That's very good of you, Chief Inspector. I appreciate it.' The old man looked up at him consideringly. 'And what marks do I get for my theory of long-distance wrong?'

Webb grinned wryly. 'Ten out of ten, sir. He's done a stretch, and Judd was the foreman of the jury that convicted him. He was convinced he'd swung them against him.'

'Excellent. Quite excellent.'

Blake said eagerly, 'So the relevant Commandment, sir, would be bearing false witness?'

'I suppose it would,' Frederick agreed, 'albeit unintentionally; I don't doubt Judd was genuinely convinced of the man's guilt. However, Chief Inspector, Baring might have a point: Paul here was saying only the other day that these rather weak, mild-mannered men can be quite ruthless, holding doggedly to their opinions when they believe they're in the right. It would have been in character if, as foreman, he'd argued forcefully against Baring.'

His face brightened. 'But to more pertinent matters; now he's under lock and key, may I go home?'

'I'm afraid not, sir, not yet. It wasn't Baring who attacked you; we're still looking for someone who takes size-nine shoes.'

Mace gave a short laugh. 'They're on to you, Paul!'

Colour flooded the young man's face as Webb glanced quickly at his feet. They certainly looked the right size, and interestingly enough the sole of one shoe, visible since Blake was sitting with his leg crossed, was of rubber.

Webb smiled noncommittally and, deciding to stay a little longer than he'd intended, seated himself on the vacant visitor's chair.

'So you're Mr Mace's researcher, Mr Blake,' he said pleasantly. 'Does that mean you do all the hard work, and he gets the glory?'

'Exactly!' Frederick confirmed.

'I wouldn't say that, Chief Inspector.' Blake's flush was fading. 'I was born curious, and nothing gives me more pleasure than unearthing facts and figures.'

'So you research full time, for other people as well?'

'No—at least, I do carry out research for other people—quite often associations, in fact—but I'm not a full-time researcher. I work at the library, and I'm also Mr Mace's secretary.'

'A busy life. You live round here, I take it?'

'Yes, I have lodgings in Sheep Street. It's convenient both for Mr Mace and the library.'

Mace put in, 'I advertised for a researcher for my last book. Paul applied, and obligingly moved over here.'

'It fitted in very well,' Blake explained. 'I'd just been offered the post at the Central Library.'

'So your family live elsewhere?'

Webb saw Mace's eyebrows lift at this persistent questioning, and the younger man flushed again.

'My parents divorced when I was a child and my father remarried. I don't see much of him these days.'

'And he lives—?' Webb persevered.

'In Oxbury.'

There was no mistaking the surprised turn of Mace's head. It seemed he'd been unaware of that.

'Is that so?' Webb said smoothly. 'No wonder you're interested in the Feathers murder. Were you living there at the time?'

'No, by then I was in the Shillingham area, at North Park Library.'

That would be checked at the earliest opportunity. Webb glanced at his watch. 'Well, I mustn't stay here chatting, I'm sure you both have a lot to discuss. Thanks for the pointer on Judd, Mr Mace. If you can do the same for Philpott, I'm sure Erlesborough police would

223

be grateful. It sticks in their craw that it's remained open for so long.'

He rose to his feet and nodded at Paul. 'Nice to have met you, Mr Blake. I presume you were asked to take your shoes along to the station? They're examining all size nines they can lay hands on, for elimination purposes.'

And without waiting for Blake's reply, he took his leave.

*   *   *

By the time Roy and the twins returned from the match, hot, sunburned and happy, Alex had showered again and changed the bed linen. As she'd stuffed sheets and pillow slips into the washing machine, she'd caught herself wishing fancifully that she could put her whole life in with them.

The boys seized gleefully on the lemonade, and she poured a glass for Roy, too.

'You should have come with us, darling,' he told her. 'As cricket matches go, it was quite exciting.'

'A contradiction in terms,' she said lightly. She found she could not meet his eyes.

'Did you go to the hospital?'

'No, it was too hot to make the effort. I'll go along this evening.'

He made no comment, and she wondered if he realized that the visit had been planned as an escape.

'Mother says he's asked for his notebooks,' she added, 'so he must be feeling better.'

'Can we go and see Grandpa?' Jack asked, wiping the lemonade from his mouth.

'I don't see why not,' Roy said. 'We can all go together tomorrow.'

Was it her imagination that he had stressed the word 'together'? She was becoming neurotic, Alex thought impatiently; this was what a guilty conscience did for you. As Patrick had hinted, hers had been a long time surfacing.

'Yes, I'm sure he'd like that,' she said.

*　　*　　*

'So congratulations are in order,' Hannah commented, as Webb handed her a glass.

'Yes; after the hold-up in locating Baring, we made pretty good time on this one.'

'But Mr Mace was right, that it wasn't connected with the other murder?'

'It was connected in that it was a copycat killing, as he'd already suggested, but Baring didn't kill Philpott, alas.'

'Still, that's not your case, is it?'

'No, thank God. By the way, I was thinking of taking Monday and Tuesday off. Perhaps we could go away for a couple of nights?'

She turned to look at him. 'You want to go away, at this stage of things?'

He swirled the liquid in his glass. 'As you

225

said, my part is finished for the moment.' He looked up, met her sceptical gaze, and grinned. 'All right, you know me too well. I *do* feel involved in the Philpott case, partly through old Mace. Still, after six years, they're not likely to wrap it up in the next four days.'

'Stranger things have happened,' Hannah said equably.

'So what do you suggest we do? Spend a couple of nights at the Oxbury Hilton?'

Hannah laughed. 'It would be a thought, if there really were any hotels.'

'There's the Five Oaks, just outside,' he reminded her. 'That's where all the Greystones parents stay.'

'Better to opt for a B and B, then we could go out for dinner each night. There are several good restaurants around.'

He looked at her in surprise. 'You're serious? About going to Oxbury?'

'Why not? It's a lovely little place; we can walk in the woods and along the river—even take a boat out if we want. And you know you wouldn't be happy going further afield just now, even if there was a chance of getting in anywhere at such short notice. My only stipulation is that you don't spend all your time detecting.'

'I couldn't if I wanted to, it wouldn't be etiquette. But there's no reason why we shouldn't sit in the odd pub and listen to what people are saying. We might come up with something useful.'

And while he was there, Webb thought to himself, he'd see what he could find out about the Blake family.

*   *   *

It was a pleasant and restful break. In Shillingham, they never went out together; Hannah's reputation had to be as unsullied as that of Caesar's wife, and Webb himself had no desire to set tongues wagging. It was fortunate indeed that they could call on each other without having to go outdoors and brave curious glances.

For the sake of propriety, Hannah even went so far as to change the ring she normally wore to her left hand. It was in three shades of gold, and could well have been a wedding band.

'If we were in our twenties or thirties, I'd brazen it out,' she defended herself when Webb laughed at her. 'But at our age we're supposed to abide by the rules. Anyway, we don't want the nice, respectable landlady looking at us askance, do we?'

Webb had looked up the name Blake in the phone book. There were only two living actually in Oxbury, and one proved to be over a shop, which he dismissed as unlikely. On the Sunday afternoon, he and Hannah strolled round to the other address, to find the windows all closed and the scorched grass overlong. Almost certainly they were away on holiday, and Webb felt safe, therefore, in stopping to speak to the man in the next-door garden.

'Excuse me, are the Blakes away?'

He straightened. 'Friends of yours, are they?'

'Friends of friends. I said I'd look them up while I was here, but it seems I'm unlucky.'

'Due back next week; we've been keeping an eye on the place. I've kept meaning to get the grass cut—bit of a giveaway—but it takes me all my time to keep our own garden straight.'

'It's their son I was hoping to see,' Webb said after a minute.

'Paul? He moved away about six years ago. Over in Ashmartin now, I believe.'

'Not married, I suppose?'

The man smiled sourly. 'You suppose right. Still, each to his own, as they say.'

Webb felt a spurt of excitement. 'That's right.' In all conscience he could say no more, and at his side Hannah was growing restive.

'Well, sorry to have missed them.'

'Who shall I say called?'

'Waters,' Webb said unblushingly. 'Douglas Waters.'

The man nodded and returned to his weeding.

'That'll keep them guessing when they get

back,' Webb commented as they continued along the road.

'Did that man mean what I think he meant?' Hannah asked curiously.

'Very probably. And you know something? It wasn't only Philpott's extra-maritals your friend Mace found out about; he was apparently anti-gay, too. I suppose it went with the macho image he had of himself. Which means that wronged husbands or lovers weren't the only people he upset.'

Hannah frowned. 'You're surely not making a connection with what that man hinted about Blake?'

'I most certainly am. He lived in Oxbury, remember, around the time of the murder. And if he really is gay, tempers could well have flared.'

Hannah stopped and stared at him. 'Oh, come on, David! If he was the killer, investigating the Feathers murder would be the last thing he'd want to do!'

'Paul Blake,' Webb said slowly, 'is an academic, a very clever young man. He enjoys his life, with its mix of books, research and writing. He worked on Mace's last book, remember, and it wasn't until this new one was well on in the planning stage that Mace took it into his head to incorporate an unsolved crime. What would you have done, in Blake's position? If, that is, he's the killer?

'To have left would have raised eyebrows, if

not suspicions, and anyway, what reason could he have given? To be plausible, he would have had to move right away from Ashmartin, which would have meant leaving the library, where he was happily settled. Much better to stay. As I said, he's very bright, and if he *is* guilty, he'll have an enormous ego, like most killers who think they've got away with it. He wouldn't consider for a moment that anyone would get on to him, particularly at this late stage. In fact, he'd enjoy the bluff. What's more,' he finished triumphantly, 'he wears size-nine shoes, as did the intruder at the Mace house.'

Hannah shook her head. 'But why on earth would he break in? He knew as much as Mace did—after all, it was he who'd supplied the information. And surely he wouldn't have *attacked* him?'

'Again, it could have been to throw everyone off the scent. I agree the attack went too far—perhaps he hit him harder than he meant to.'

'But wasn't the dog there? You told me Mace said it growled. It wouldn't have growled at Paul Blake, it knew him.'

'So the case rests on the dog that growled in the night, rather than the one that didn't? Actually, though, if he was lurking in the dark where he wasn't expected to be, it might have growled anyway.'

They walked in silence for a while. Then Hannah asked, 'What put you on to Blake in the first place? Just the fact that he wears size-

230

nine shoes?'

'And because he looked most uncomfortable when comment was passed on them. And because Mace obviously didn't know he'd lived in Oxbury. And because he's so close to Mace. Anyway, I'm not "on" to him, I'm merely considering him for the part, like everyone else. Though if he turns out to be gay, it could hand us the motive on a plate.'

'So what are you going to do?'

'Have a word with Ted Ferris. And possibly Good; get him to make inquiries at Blake's digs. It wouldn't do any harm.'

'Right, that's settled.' Hannah took his arm. 'And now, please may we get on with our holiday?'

*   *   *

Edwina had declined Gillian and Hugh's invitation to stay with them while Frederick was in hospital. After four weeks touring Canada, she was only just getting used to her own bed again and had no wish to leave it.

Also, she conceded privately, she did not want Gillian to detect her fear, which she was sure to do if they were in close contact. Fear not for herself—being alone in the large house held no terrors for her; she had Goldie for company, even if he hadn't acquitted himself too well in Frederick's hour of need.

No, the fear was for Frederick, and for Alex,

231

who seemed increasingly unhappy. Edwina had seen her briefly yesterday afternoon; she'd been on the point of leaving the hospital when the four of them arrived, and for the first time, Alex had refused to meet her eyes.

What with everything that had been going on, Edwina had still not had the chance to ask Gilly about her visit to Alex. It suddenly struck her that, despite the family crises, it was odd that Gilly, knowing how concerned she was, hadn't phoned her.

Did that mean she'd found out something, and didn't know how to tell her mother? Or that she'd not found out anything, so hadn't bothered to phone? Or, most disturbing of all, that Alex had sworn her to secrecy?

Then there was Frederick. He was progressing well—there were no worries on that score—but the hornet's nest he'd stirred up still hadn't died down. A man had been charged with the latest murder, but, sinisterly, it was reported that 'he'd been eliminated from inquiries concerning the Feathers investigation.' So that killer was still on the loose.

She wished passionately that Frederick could come home in safety, without the fear of some maniac doing him further harm. How much longer would this topsy-turvy existence go on? She'd had more than enough of it.

And there was another thing: something seemed to have happened between Frederick

232

and Paul Blake. Paul had called yesterday morning to ask her to take some notebooks to the hospital, and he'd seemed on edge, refusing to meet her eyes. But when she mentioned it to Frederick later, all he'd say was that there'd been a misunderstanding and Paul had called back later to apologize. The matter was closed, and there was no point in discussing it any further.

From his set face, Edwina doubted very much that the matter was closed, but it was obvious he didn't want to discuss it with her, and she felt a little hurt at being excluded.

'I wish Chief Inspector Good was in charge of the Feathers case,' she'd told him. 'It didn't take him long to find his murderer, and the Erlesborough police have been dragging their feet for six years. I can't say I've much faith in them.'

Frederick had grunted. 'Actually, I'd be quite disappointed if the police beat me to it. I'm still hoping to pin down the killer by means of his motive.'

'What I'm frightened of,' she'd replied grimly, 'is the killer pinning *you* down.'

*   *   *

Webb and Hannah went to a different pub each evening for their pre-dinner drink, but the name of Trevor Philpott was never mentioned in their hearing, and, mindful of his

233

promise, Webb did not engage anyone in conversation.

When he got home, he'd ring Ted Ferris and ask how the inquiry was going. Admittedly the ground had all been covered before, but with the Judd connection, Erlesborough now had the bit between their teeth and were likely, Webb thought, with a glorious disregard for metaphors, to be pulling out all the stops.

In the meantime, it was good to relax with Hannah in this quiet country place. They had, as planned, walked in the woods and taken a boat out on the Kittle, visited several antique shops, where Hannah had bought a few trinkets, and eaten well on the three evenings of their stay. He felt pleasantly rested and at peace with the world.

Now, it was their last night, and what was more, they'd have to leave at seven in the morning to be back in Shillingham in time for his shift.

'Enjoyed the break?' he asked Hannah, as she nestled against him in the old-fashioned bed.

'Very much. Just shows what fun you can have in your own backyard.'

'Tell you what: if we crack the Feathers case, we'll celebrate with a really slap-up holiday abroad somewhere. How about that?'

She yawned. 'Will I have to wait another six years?'

He smiled in the darkness. 'You might, at

234

that. I'm not working on that one.'

'But Frederick Mace is!' she teased him. 'My money's on him!'

CHAPTER THIRTEEN

Webb's first call on Tuesday morning was to Harry Good.

'Harry, I know you're resting on your laurels at the moment, but would you do something for me? Have you met Mace's assistant, Paul Blake?'

'Not personally, but he was seen along with other known contacts after the attack.'

'Presumably whoever saw him noted that he takes size nine shoes? And that he comes from Oxbury? And that he might possibly be homosexual?'

Interest quickened in Good's voice. 'Exactly what are you saying, Dave?'

'Nothing specific, but various things occurred to me over the weekend. For one thing, Mace was there when I wormed the Oxbury connection out of Blake, and I'd swear he hadn't known about it. Wouldn't you say that's odd, when they're working together on an Oxbury murder? Also, Blake's neighbour inferred that he was homosexual, and we're told Philpott indulged in a spot of gay-bashing. Suppose his death was retaliation that, perhaps, went further than intended? I know it's a long shot, but at this stage we have to grab any straws that present themselves.

'Of course, even if Blake did kill Philpott, it could have been for an entirely different reason. I just think he's worth looking into.'

Good sounded doubtful. 'As you say, it's a long shot all right. You seriously think he's a suspect?'

'Only in so far as everyone is, until we nail the killer. I'm about to phone Ted Ferris, but it would help if you could organize a bit of snooping on your patch, perhaps give us more to go on.'

'Of course, anything we can do.'

'Blake's in digs in Sheep Street; perhaps a WPC could chat up the landlady?'

'OK, Dave, I'll lay it on. Anything else?'

'A tail mightn't be a bad idea, but it would have to be a discreet one; he's a bright lad.'

'What exactly are we looking for?'

'Where he spends his spare time, who his friends are, that kind of thing.'

'Will do. I'll get back to you.'

Webb's next call was to Ferris.

'Jammy bastard, aren't you?' his Erlesborough counterpart greeted him.

'Do I take that as congratulations, Ted?'

'I suppose so, but it's pretty galling when you lot charge someone inside two weeks, and we're still plodding along six years later.'

'Well, it's possible I might have a lead for

you, though at the moment only a tenuous one. You've been following the attack on Frederick Mace?'

'Too right; it's thanks to the old boy that we learned about Philpott's past.'

'Has it opened up any new lines?'

'Not so far, but we have hopes. There's a couple, friends of the Philpotts, who might be able to shed a bit of light, but as luck would have it they're away on holiday.'

'Well, for what it's worth, here's another possibility.' And Webb repeated what he'd told Good.

'You're surely not suggesting Philpott was bisexual? Anyone less likely—'

'Could be he protested too much, but no, I hadn't thought that far. And I might be way off-beam, it's only an idea.'

'I gather it wasn't Mace who put you on to this?'

'Lord, no.'

'Should he be warned?'

'He's safe enough at the moment, and we can't queer the man's pitch, if you'll forgive the expression, without anything more to go on. It's not a crime to wear size-nine shoes and come from Oxbury.'

'Well, that's a relief, or our cells would be overflowing!'

'Good luck, Ted. I'll keep in touch.'

*   *   *

Hannah had spent most of the morning searching for her fountain pen, and it wasn't until she tried to think back to the last time she'd used it that she realized she must have left it at school. Since she didn't want to be without it for the rest of the holidays, she decided to go straight over and retrieve it.

As she walked down the hill towards the school, she was thinking of the weekend just behind her. It had been pleasant to walk freely along the road with David, without worrying who might see them. She wondered whether he had put the inquiries he'd mentioned into motion, and what would be the result of them. Since Philpott's killer, whoever he was, apparently roamed the county, it would be a relief to know he was behind bars.

She turned into Montpellier Crescent and skirted the railed gardens in its centre, an oasis of coolness under the trees. The residents of the crescent, including the school, had keys to it, and Hannah sometimes went to sit there during her lunch hour, when the school grounds were noisy with girls.

Ashbourne awaited her at the far end and she pushed open the gates and made her way up the long drive, past the banks of evergreens and the deserted tennis courts. She loved this place, it was a very important part of her life, and she hoped fervently she would never feel pressured into leaving it.

As she rounded the last curve of the drive, she caught a merging flash of red and blue as two figures disappeared round the far corner of the house. Hannah paused, frowning. Could it have been the gardeners? They were the only people who'd any business here during the holidays.

She quickened her step and set off in pursuit, coming to an abrupt halt as she rounded the corner of the building, for the couple ahead had stopped to look at a plant and were only yards in front of her. A man and a woman, they were standing hand in hand with their backs to her, and Hannah saw with a sense of disbelief that the woman was Gwen.

Some sound, or possibly the intensity of her gaze, alerted them, for they turned together, disengaging their hands and regarding her in considerable embarrassment. Gwen's face had flushed as scarlet as her dress, and Hannah thought inconsequentially how pretty she looked.

Since neither of them seemed capable of speech, Hannah said awkwardly, 'I'm so sorry to intrude. I came to get my fountain pen, I'd no idea—'

'Of course you hadn't.' Gwen gestured towards her companion. 'Hannah, may I introduce Professor Cameron, whom I met in Canada? Bruce, this is Hannah James, my deputy.'

Hannah dragged her eyes from Gwen to the

man at her side. Slightly shorter than Gwen, he was of stocky build, with a shock of rough grey hair and a sunburnt, intelligent face. His eyes, now looking at her with interest, were the same deep blue as his sports shirt.

He came forward with his hand out. 'Delighted to meet you, ma'am. I've heard a lot about you.'

Which was a comment she couldn't reciprocate. There was a brief pause, then Hannah said hurriedly, 'Well, I won't disturb you, I'll just collect—'

'No, Hannah, wait. I—think we need to talk.'

The professor took charge. 'You ladies would find this easier if I weren't with you. Miss James, I was just saying to Gwendoline that I hoped you would join us for dinner this evening; perhaps I might extend the invitation in person?'

Hannah, completely at a loss—who was this man?—murmured confusedly, 'Well, that's very kind of you—'

'Shall we say seven-thirty at my hotel, the King's Head on Gloucester Circus?' He had the usual North American difficulty with the name. 'I'll wait for you in the foyer.'

He turned to Gwen, tongue-tied beside him. 'I'll call you later, my dear.' And with an old-fashioned little bow, he left them, disappearing round the corner of the building.

Hannah said forcefully, 'Gwen, what on

earth's going on?'

'Oh Hannah, I'm sorry. I've handled everything very badly, but Bruce's arrival was totally unexpected, I swear. He rang me from Heathrow on Saturday, the day after your supper party. I did try to phone you yesterday, but there was no reply.'

'But who *is* he? You've never mentioned him.'

'There was no reason to. I didn't—Look, let's walk, shall we? I'm too restless to sit still, and it might make things easier.'

Hannah fell into step beside her, her mind spinning.

'Firstly, I really am sorry I blurted out about the headship offer on Friday. I should have told you first. Put it down to that excellent wine you gave us.'

'It doesn't matter.' Hannah brushed aside the subject which had loomed over her for the last few days, in her impatience to return to Bruce Cameron.

'But I didn't keep this from you, honestly. There was—simply nothing to tell. I met Bruce at a drinks party soon after I arrived in Canada. He lectures at Macmillan University and is a specialist on medieval law.'

'That must come in handy.'

Gwen smiled fleetingly. 'I liked him at once. I learned that his wife had died three years ago, that he was interested in music and walking and sketching—'

'In fact,' Hannah interrupted drily, 'all things that interest you.'

'Yes, exactly. So we saw quite a lot of each other over the next months. But Hannah—I must emphasize this—it was totally platonic.'

'And you didn't want it to be?'

She was remembering their conversation the evening after Gwen's return from Canada. Gwen had asked if she'd ever regretted not marrying, and when Hannah had handed back the question, she'd admitted to not being sure. And, Hannah remembered with embarrassment, she'd teased her about falling for a Mountie.

'I don't know what I wanted,' Gwen was answering frankly. 'I'd long ago given up all thoughts of marriage, convinced myself that my career fulfilled all my needs. There's never been a man in my life, Hannah, you know that. I'm aware that there is in yours; if you remember, you confided in me a few years ago, when you were having problems. But I've no idea who he is, and I don't want to know. I'm just glad for you.'

Hannah took her arm and squeezed it.

'So I was dismayed when I found myself thinking more and more about Bruce, and dreading the time when I'd have to leave. Then, out of the blue, came the offer of the headship at Layton High. In one sense it seemed the answer to my prayers, but in another it was impossible. Although I enjoyed

Bruce's company, I was becoming increasingly nervous of betraying my feelings for him, and he'd never so much as hinted at any for me.'

They came to a halt, gazing out across the playing fields to the junior school against the far wall of the grounds.

'So I told them I'd consider the offer, shook hands with Bruce, said it had been nice knowing him, and came home. Since when,' she added honestly, 'I've been thoroughly miserable.'

'I knew something was wrong,' Hannah said softly. 'So what brought the professor over?'

'It seems he told a close friend of his feelings for me, and as luck would have it, the wife of this friend thought she'd detected signs that I cared for him. They both persuaded him to come over and—try his luck.'

'He didn't waste much time; you've only been back two weeks.' She looked sideways at her friend's rapt face, gazing into the distance with eyes narrowed against the sun.

'Dare I ask what happened when he arrived?'

Gwen smiled. 'After a certain amount of preamble, he told me that he—he loved me, and asked me to marry him.'

'Oh, Gwen! And of course you said yes?'

Gwen turned impulsively towards her. 'Was it wrong of me, Hannah? Is it selfish, at my age, to give up everything I have here and fly off without a backward glance, like a—a GI bride? You saw how delighted Mother was to be home again; how can I tell her—or Bea—that I won't be there much longer?'

'Of course it's not selfish,' Hannah said roundly. 'And your mother was perfectly happy with Beatrice. The fact that John's a doctor is a positive advantage, with her eyesight not too good. I'm sure *they* wouldn't mind the arrangement being permanent.'

And perhaps not too permanent, Hannah thought privately; Mrs Rutherford was in her late eighties and her health was failing.

'Look,' she went on positively, 'this couldn't be more perfect. You're not even being asked to give up your career. You have a brand-new challenge out there in Canada, and you'll have a husband who's also in education to help and advise you. What could be better?'

When Gwen didn't reply, she added, 'When and where are you getting married?'

'Here, as soon as possible. We want a quiet wedding—only a few close friends. We're hoping Bruce's will fly over.'

'Then what?'

'Well, the vacancy won't be for a year, as I told you, and in any case I have to give twelve months' notice myself. So he'll arrange a sabbatical and stay over here with me, and I'll continue at Ashbourne till the end of next summer term. After which, if the gods are good, it will pass to you.'

'Gwen, I'm so happy for you. And I look

forward to getting to know your Bruce better over dinner this evening.'

By common consent, they turned and started to walk back towards the main building.

*　　*　　*

WPC Julie Dean, in shorts, T-shirt and flip-flops, rang the bell of number seven Sheep Street, an eye on the notice in the window.

The door was opened by a motherly-looking woman in an apron. 'Yes, dear?'

'I see you have a vacancy,' Julie said.

The woman looked her up and down. 'For yourself, is it?'

'Yes. It would only be for a few days; I've come over to see a friend, but she can't put me up.'

'I think that would be all right. Would you like to see the room?'

'Please.'

'My name's Mrs Kershaw,' the woman said as she went up the stairs ahead of Julie. 'And yours?'

'Julie Dean.'

'Well, Julie, the rule is no visitors in the bedrooms. There's a parlour downstairs where you can entertain friends.'

'That's fine by me.'

They had reached the square landing. Mrs Kershaw opened the door on to a small bedroom, only just large enough to accommodate single bed, wardrobe and dressing table. It would, Julie felt, have been difficult to entertain anyone here, even if it had been allowed.

'This'll be fine,' she said. At least it was clean, and the bed looked comfortable. 'Is anyone else staying here?' she asked.

'Yes, I've a long-term lodger, Mr Blake. Ever such a nice gentleman, very quiet.'

'How long is long-term?' Julie inquired smilingly.

'Oh, he's been with me a couple of years now. What I meant to say is that this room, being on the small side, is for occasional short-term visitors, though of course, if you need to stay on, there'd be no problem.'

They went back down the stairs and, apparently having accepted Julie as one of the family, Mrs Kershaw offered her a cup of coffee. She accepted with alacrity and followed her new landlady into the kitchen.

'What does Mr Blake do?' she asked idly, taking the chair indicated at the table.

'He's a librarian,' Mrs Kershaw told her, her voice full of respect, 'but he also works for Mr Mace—you know, the writer.'

'The man who was mugged recently?'

'That's right, dear. Terrible business, I must say.'

'It must have been a shock for Mr Blake.'

'Yes,' Mrs Kershaw agreed, placing two

mugs of coffee on the table, 'specially coming right on top of his own accident.'

Julie looked up, policewoman's ears pricked. 'He had an accident?'

'That he did, the same night. Came back in a right state, I can tell you.'

'He was mugged too?' She fixed wide, innocent eyes on her landlady.

'Oh no, nothing like that. Slipped and fell on his way home. Nasty graze on his arm, and he was quite shaken.'

Which, thought WPC Dean, would certainly be of interest to the governor.

*   *   *

In Oxbury, the investigation into the death of Trevor Philpott was proceeding with dogged determination but not much joy. It wasn't that those questioned refused to cooperate; most of them were only too ready to repeat what they'd said in their original statements six years before—in many cases, almost word for word. No doubt their stories had been retold to friends and acquaintances so often over the years that the tellers knew them almost by heart. At any rate, nothing new emerged.

At Ward and Johnson, the estate agent's where Philpott had worked, the story of his happy marriage still prevailed, and despite intensive questioning, those who had known him maintained they'd never heard anything to make them doubt it.

And then, just when it seemed to the police that stalemate had been reached, their luck finally changed, with a phone call from DCI Horn in Broadminster.

'Good news, Ted!' he greeted Ferris. 'That couple you wanted us to contact, the Hartwells: we got their holiday address from their neighbours—they're up in the wilds of Scotland—and the local bobby's been round to see them.'

Ferris leant forward, gripping the phone. 'Did Philpott name the women?'

'He apparently reeled off half a dozen, but Hartwell only remembers one, because he knew her. It was the landlady of the local pub, the Stag—Mrs Vera Chadwick.'

Ferris leaned back in his chair, letting out his held breath. 'Foggy, I owe you one. With luck, this could be just what we're looking for.'

He pushed back his chair and strode into the outer office. 'Come on, Rob,' he told his startled sergeant, 'we're off for a pub lunch in Oxbury.'

*   *   *

The Stag was crowded with lunchtime drinkers and the two detectives, having ordered a couple of pints and two ploughman's, were content to position themselves at a table opposite the bar and watch the couple serving

248

behind it, whose identity had already been established by the bantering comments of the locals.

The woman was, Ferris estimated, in her early forties. Her face was flushed, both from the heat of the room and from her steady and unremitting work, but she kept up a cheerful stream of chat as she took the orders and served her thirsty customers.

Ferris studied her critically, trying to see her as Philpott had. Yes, she'd got something going for her; the hair which stuck to her damp forehead was blonde and curling, her face roundly pretty, her eyes wide and blue. More pertinently, some of the looks she flashed at those leaning on the bar were what Ferris's dad would have described as 'come-hither', and her chat, from what he caught of it, was decidedly on the risqué side. He was willing to bet she hadn't wanted for consolation when Trevor Philpott died.

Munching on a pickled onion, he turned his attention to her husband. Dick Chadwick was large in every way—tall, broad, with a huge stomach which presumably went with the job. He seemed a jovial man, his face as red and shining as his wife's, his hair thinning on top but still bushy at the sides. Did he, Ferris wondered, know of his wife's carryings on, and if so, did he care? He certainly didn't look like a murderer, but unfortunately that was nothing to go by.

The two men sat on until the crowd had thinned and dispersed to return to farm, shop or office and the day's work. Then, Ferris slid out from behind the table and strolled over to the bar.

'Mrs Vera Chadwick?' he asked, producing his warrant card, and saw her eyes widen. 'DCI Ferris from Erlesborough. I wonder if I could have a word?'

'My goodness!' She gave a gasping little laugh. 'What have I done this time?'

She flashed a look at her husband, busy wiping glasses further down the bar. 'Can you hold the fort, Dick, while I speak to these gentlemen?'

He nodded without even looking round—possibly used to such a request. Vera Chadwick lifted the counter and came round the bar, then, beckoning to the policemen, led them down a tiled passageway to a small snug at the back of the building. It was dark in there, the window being overgrown with honeysuckle which almost obscured the glass.

'Right, gents, what can I do for you?'

At close quarters, there was an undeniable animal attraction about her. Her blouse clung to her hot body, outlining full breasts, and her bare brown legs were thrust into none too clean sandals, but the scent of warm flesh which she exuded was by no means unpleasant.

Ferris cleared his throat. 'We'd like to ask you about Mr Trevor Philpott.'

250

She blinked, her lashes, sticky with mascara, screening her eyes for a moment. Then, looking up at him, she said, 'Again? I've already told your chaps. He only came in from time to time—he wasn't a regular.'

'He was something else, though, wasn't he, Mrs Chadwick?'

She gnawed briefly on her lip, then, abandoning dissemblance, flashed him a conspiratorial smile. 'Well, you're a big boy, Chief Inspector, you know how things are.'

Ferris was aware of his sergeant's twitching mouth, and to his annoyance felt his colour rise.

'You were having an affair with him?' he demanded.

'If you want to put it that way. We'd a thing going, yes.'

'What about your husband? Did he know about it?'

'No, no one did, which was what made it special.'

'You are quite sure of that, Mrs Chadwick? It's very important.'

'I'm positive. Trev insisted on absolute secrecy. That's why he wouldn't come here regular.'

'Are you aware he arranged to meet someone here on the night he died?'

She nodded sombrely. 'We were told at the time. But they must have met outside, because Trev certainly never came in that night. Dick and I can both swear to that.'

Which, Ferris thought, gave Chadwick a cast-iron alibi. He flicked a look at his sergeant, unobtrusively taking notes. 'How long did the affair last?'

She shrugged. 'A couple of years, on and off, but it wasn't heavy. We both had other irons in the fire, as you might say.'

Ferris tensed. 'He was seeing other women at the same time?'

'Yeah—why not? I'm not the jealous type.'

'Did he tell you who they were?'

She shook her head. ' "No names, no pack drill," he used to say. He went for married women, though, I know that—so they'd have their own reasons for keeping it quiet.'

'Did you ever guess, from what he said, who they might have been?'

She shrugged. 'I wasn't that interested.'

'But we are, Mrs Chadwick.'

She met his eyes, and he saw understanding come. 'Oh, I get you.'

'Please try to think. Is there anything at all you remember? Someone whose husband found out, or anything like that?'

She frowned, thinking back. 'Come to think of it, there was one. He was in a right state about her. Not long before he died, it must have been. Someone in the office where he worked—it surprised me, because he told me once he never messed with anyone there. I remember him saying, "I broke my own rule,

252

Vera, and look where it's got me."'

'Did he say *where* it had got him?' Ferris demanded urgently.

'Not really. Just that there'd been an upset, and the girl had left.'

'And this happened shortly before he was killed?'

'Yeah. Come to think of it, that was probably the last time I saw him.' Her eyes filled suddenly with tears.

'Thank you, Mrs Chadwick. You've been an enormous help.'

Out on the pavement, Ferris pulled out his mobile phone. 'What's the number of Ward and Johnson, Rob?'

He dialled it as the sergeant read it out, and was put through to the manager.

'Mr Laycock, this is vitally important. Have you any means of looking up your records and finding out who among your staff left just before Mr Philpott was killed? . . . Yes, I'll hold on.'

The wait seemed interminable. It was hot in the afternoon sunshine, but neither Ferris nor his sergeant was aware of it, nor of the life of the little town continuing round about them. Tense, hardly daring to hope, they waited, and at last the manager's voice came back.

'As far as I can see, Chief Inspector, one of our clerks left in October that year—Richard Simpson. That seems—Just a moment, Sandra's remembered something.'

253

He covered the mouthpiece with his hand and Ferris, seething with impatience, could hear muffled voices behind it. Then Laycock's came clearly again. 'She says one of the typists left about then, too, if that's of any interest. Her name was Zoë Knowles.'

CHAPTER FOURTEEN

The woman in the doorway looked at them blankly.

'Mrs Knowles?' Ferris asked.

'Who?'

His heart dropped like a stone. 'Are you Mrs Knowles, ma'am?'

'Oh—no, the name's Fielding. The Knowleses moved away years ago.'

Ferris closed his eyes briefly in frustration. 'Have you any idea where they went?'

'Over to the east of the county, I think. Yes, that's right—Honeyford. We drove through it once, and my husband said, "This is where the Knowleses moved to." Quiet sort of place.'

'Thank you, you've been most helpful.'

Ferris hurried back to the car and, sliding inside, took out his phone again.

'Dave? It's Ted. I'm in Oxbury, and we could be on to something: girl by the name of Zoë Knowles, might have been involved with Philpott. She moved from here to Honeyford

254

some years ago. That's on your patch, isn't it?'

'Yes. What have you got on her?'

'Nothing, really. It's a convoluted trail—I'll explain when I see you.'

'You're coming over?'

'You bet we are. Straight away.'

'Right, I'll see if I can track her down and meet you there. How long will it take you?'

'About an hour and a quarter, I'd say.'

'I'll wait outside the Swan—it's the first pub as you enter the village.'

'Thanks, Dave, we're on our way.'

* * *

It was four-fifteen when Ferris's car drew up behind Webb's outside the Swan. Webb got out and walked back.

'We've located her, Ted. Girl and her mother live in Swing-Gate Lane.'

Ferris frowned. 'Her mother? No husband?'

'No, Zoë's the daughter, according to the newsagent across the road there. While I was waiting I went over for a paper and engaged him in a bit of chat. No father either; died when she was an infant.'

'Then who the hell are we looking for?'

'You tell me.'

Ferris swore softly. 'Do you know if she's home?'

'Someone is; there's a car in the drive. We don't want to alarm her by crowding her out, though; I suggest we stop just short of the house and the two sergeants stay in the cars.'

'Fine; you lead the way, then.'

They set off in convoy. Jackson turned down the first road on the left and after a hundred yards or so drew to a halt. Seconds later, Ferris's car stopped behind them.

The two senior detectives got out. The sun had disappeared and there was an oppressive air to the day, as though all the oxygen had been used up. As they turned in the gate, Webb saw that the house was little more than a cottage, chocolate-box pretty in its Broadshire stone, with a steeply pitched roof and, literally, roses round the door. They walked up the path and rang the bell.

The door was flung open by a pale, fair woman in her thirties, who appeared taken aback to see them.

'Oh—I'm sorry, I thought it would be the doctor.'

'Police, ma'am.'

Before Webb could continue, her eyes widened and she exclaimed, 'It's not my mother, is it? Nothing's—happened?'

'No, no, Miss Knowles.' He paused. 'I take it you *are* Miss Knowles—Miss Zoë Knowles?'

'Yes, that's right.' Puzzled, she looked from one face to the other.

'Chief Inspectors Ferris and Webb.' They both held up their cards.

She said tentatively, 'How do you do?'

256

'May we come inside, please?'

Still bewildered, she stood to one side and they went directly into a charming living-room. Obviously genuine old beams criss-crossed a low ceiling, and most of one wall was taken up by a stone fireplace, the grate of which was masked by a basket of flowers.

The table and dresser, of a rich, dark wood Webb couldn't identify, were polished to a high sheen, and the comfortable easy chairs were covered in chintz. No attempt had been made to double-glaze the small, diamond-paned windows, and a staircase went up from one side of the room. Webb felt a twinge of envy; he could comfortably live here himself.

He nodded to Ferris, who began without preamble, 'Miss Knowles, we're looking into the death of Mr Trevor Philpott. I wonder—

He broke off in consternation as she swayed, her eyes flickering. Webb moved quickly forward and guided her into a chair.

'We don't mean to distress you, Zoë, but we have to ask you some questions.' He hoped the use of her first name would reassure her, but her deepening pallor showed no signs of improving. 'You did know Mr Philpott, didn't you?'

'We—worked in the same office.' He had to bend down to hear her.

'But there was more to it than that, wasn't there?'

'I don't know what you mean!' She rose

257

unsteadily to her feet, holding on to the chair for support. 'I'd be grateful if you'd go now. My mother—'

'Did you have an affair with Mr Philpott, Miss Knowles?' Ferris this time.

She gave a little moan, both hands going to her mouth.

'Shortly before he was killed?' Ferris persisted. 'Your boyfriend wouldn't have liked that, would he?'

'My —?' She stared at them with total lack of comprehension.

From beyond the open window came the crunching of footsteps on the path, the door opened, and a tall, fair man came into the house, stopping short on seeing the tableau before him. Right on cue, Webb thought, regarding him with interest.

'What the hell's going on?' he demanded.

'Patrick—oh, Patrick, thank God!' Zoë's knees began to buckle. The man caught hold of her, his arm encircling her protectively.

'What is this? Who are you, and what are you doing in my sister's house?'

The detectives exchanged a significant look, and Webb released his breath in a long sigh.

'You're Mr Knowles, sir?'

'Of course I am. More to the point, who are you?'

'DCIs Ferris and Webb. We're looking into the murder of Trevor Philpott.'

There was total silence. Then Patrick

Knowles said, 'Oh, my God.'

Zoë had begun to weep silently. 'Make them go away,' she begged.

'We have reason to believe, sir, that your sister had a relationship with him. Is that correct?'

Knowles didn't answer. His face was now as white as his sister's.

'Did she?' Webb repeated.

'All right, damn you, yes, she did . . . And I bet she wasn't the only one.'

'But perhaps she took it harder than the rest?'

'Look, you can see this is distressing her. She's not well, and added to that, our mother is seriously ill in hospital.'

'I'm sorry, sir. If you'd like to make arrangements for your sister, we're quite agreeable to hearing the story from you.'

Patrick held his eyes for a long moment. Then he said, 'I'll ring my wife. She can be here in fifteen minutes.'

He gently lowered his sister into her chair, and disappeared through one of the doors opening off the living-room. They heard him say, 'Sonia, there's an emergency. Can you come to Honeyford at once, and take charge of Zoë? . . . What? No, it's not Mother. Just get here as soon as you can, for God's sake.'

Faced with a fifteen-minute delay, Webb moved restlessly to the window, in time to see a short, dark man turn into the gateway and walk briskly up the path. Webb recognized him from a case in the area two years ago; it was Dr Pratt.

The doctor gave a token tap on the door and came straight in, looking in surprise at the gathering.

Knowles greeted him with relief. 'Doctor, thank God you're here! My sister's not well, and I have to speak to these gentlemen; could you possibly —?'

The doctor's eyes went to the detectives and he gave Webb a brief nod. 'Of course, she can come and rest in the surgery until you're ready for her.'

'I take it there's no news on my mother?'

'Nothing significant. I called in because I promised your sister I would, but there's really nothing to report.'

He helped Patrick raise Zoë to her feet and between them they guided her down the path. Webb kept an eye on Knowles through the window, phone at the ready in case he needed to alert Jackson, but the man returned almost at once.

'The doctor lives next door but one. She'll be all right for the moment. Look, I need a drink. Can I get you anything?'

'No, thank you, sir.'

He went to the sideboard, removed a whisky bottle from one of its cupboards and poured a shot into a crystal tumbler.

'Philpott was a rat,' he said unemotionally,

'and whoever killed him deserves a medal.'

Ferris resumed his questioning. 'What happened, sir?'

'He made a play for my sister. She didn't realize his game—she's always been immature for her age—and she really fell for him. He spun her the usual line, he'd divorce his wife, all the rest of it. Even so, she still refused to sleep with him. So,' Knowles said deliberately, sitting down in the chair his sister had vacated and staring into his glass, 'he took her out in his car and raped her.'

The words hung in the charming room, brutal and alien. 'I'm very sorry to hear that,' Ferris said quietly. 'Why didn't you report it?'

'How could we bloody report it?' Knowles's voice was savage. 'What do you think it would have done to her, to my mother, if it had all come out in court? Wasn't it bad enough that she had to go through it once, without bringing it all up again?' He wiped a hand across his face. 'Then we realized she was pregnant. We arranged an immediate abortion, but it was all too much for her and she had a breakdown. She's—never been the same since.'

Yet again there were sounds on the path outside, and this time the door burst open to admit a tall, slim woman with shoulder-length brown hair. She, too, stopped short on seeing them.

'Patrick —?' she said hesitantly.

'These men are detectives, Sonia.'

She frowned. 'But—Zoë?'

'Dr Pratt has taken her. No'—at her exclamation—'she's all right, but she wasn't up to the—questioning.'

'Questioning?' Mrs Knowles repeated, looking from one to another.

'These gentlemen, my dear, are on the point of asking me if I murdered Trevor Philpott.'

Sonia Knowles gasped, but Ferris forestalled her. 'Mr Knowles, I think I should caution you that—'

He interrupted with an impatient gesture. 'Save your breath; I'm not making any statement, other than to say categorically that I did *not*.'

'All the same, sir, I'm afraid it will be necessary for you to accompany us to the station. A statement will be required, even if it's only to repeat what you've already told us.'

'What *have* you told them, Patrick?' Sonia demanded urgently.

Knowles looked at her briefly, then away. 'That Philpott raped Zoë and she had to have an abortion.'

She stared at him in horror. 'Is that what her illness was all about?'

'She had a breakdown afterwards.'

'Why didn't you tell me?'

Why indeed, thought Webb. 'What size shoes do you take, Mr Knowles?' he asked conversationally.

'What?' Knowles turned to him with a

262

frown.

'Your shoes; what size are they?'

'Nines, though I can't see—' He broke off as, patently, he began to see.

'Do you possess a pair with rubber soles?'

Knowles was about to deny it, but his wife cried, 'What have Patrick's shoes got to do with anything? Is it now a crime to own rubber soles?'

Ferris said tonelessly, 'Whoever broke in to the Mace house was wearing them. We'll need to examine yours, Mr Knowles.'

Sonia looked from him to Patrick's wooden face. 'You can't seriously believe my husband would *break in* to the Maces' house?' she said incredulously. 'They're *friends* of ours—I've known them most of my life.'

'He was getting too close, wasn't he?' Webb remarked, ignoring her. 'He'd worked out by some method of his own what type of man Philpott had been, contrary to received opinion. And he stated in public that he'd been killed, not by one of those he'd hurt directly, but by someone avenging her. We assumed he meant a husband or lover, but a brother would have an equally strong motive. Especially,' Webb added, remembering the newsagent's words, 'one who'd felt responsible for his sister from childhood.'

Sonia Knowles reached blindly behind her for a chair and lowered herself into it.

'My goodness,' Knowles said gratingly, 'you

263

have been doing your homework. Well, Mr Webb, or whatever your name is, in this country we're still innocent until proved guilty, so you can theorize all you like. Even if I *had* killed Philpott, there's nothing that could link me with it.'

'Perhaps I should warn you that when we get to the station, we'll be requiring a blood or saliva sample.'

Knowles's knuckles whitened on the arm of his chair. 'Why?'

'Because, Mr Knowles, we're arresting you in connection with two crimes which we believe are linked, the murder of Trevor Philpott and the attack on Mr Mace. And a couple of hairs other than his own were found on Mr Mace's clothing.'

*   *   *

On the way back to Shillingham, Webb phoned Harry Good from the car to inform him of developments.

'Well, he's a dark horse!' Good commented. 'I've never even heard of him!'

'You'll be hearing a lot more, believe me. Ted Ferris and I are on our way to interview him now. Have you any specific questions you want answering on Mace's attack?'

'Nothing more than you'd ask yourself. Come back to me as soon as you have a result.'

'You can bet on it.'

By the time Knowles had had his sample taken and been escorted to the interview room, the fight had gone out of him. He even declined the services of a solicitor. They'd left Sonia in tears at the cottage, having been instructed by Patrick to collect her sister-in-law from the doctor and to stay with her.

'But when will you be back?' she'd cried desperately.

Knowles had climbed into Ferris's car without answering.

Now, seated across the table in the interview room, Webb thought how exhausted the man looked. Until the Judd murder, he must have thought he'd got away with it. In fact, right up until Frederick Mace started declaiming his theories on the Ten Commandments. A very different character from Baring, this one, with a totally different motive, as Mace had recognized.

Ferris switched on the tape and went through the preliminaries.

As he stopped speaking, there was silence. Knowles was sitting motionless, his head bent, staring at the pitted table in front of him.

'When you're ready, sir.'

He raised his head and looked at Webb. 'Was that on the level, about the hairs on Mace's clothes?'

265

Webb nodded, then said gently, 'Wouldn't it be a relief to get it off your chest?'

Knowles spread his hands in a gesture of resignation. 'All right, Chief Inspector, you win. But before I say anything, I must make it clear neither my mother nor Zoë has the slightest inkling I was involved in Philpott's death. They simply thought he'd got his just deserts.

'The irony is that I never meant to kill him anyway. My intention was to take him somewhere he couldn't just walk away from, but would have to hear me out. I meant to tell him what I thought of him, punch him on the jaw, then dump him and leave him to find his own way home. I hoped it would be a lesson to him.'

'Perhaps,' Ferris suggested, 'you'd better start at the beginning.'

Knowles sighed, thinking back. 'We'd an awful job finding out what had happened. Zoë arrived home in hysterics and wouldn't stop crying. When we did get it out of her, I wanted to report Philpott, either to you or his manager, but she wouldn't hear of it—swore she'd kill herself if anyone found out what had happened. So, officially, my hands were tied, but I was damned if he was going to get away with it. At the very least I wanted reimbursement for her medical expenses.

'So I pretended I had a house for sale, in a location that was difficult to find. I suggested picking him up outside the Stag and driving him out there. He was quite amenable.

'It was November, a cold, foggy evening. I drove out into the country, and turned down a rutted lane I'd earmarked when driving past. Then I stopped the car and we got out—as I thought, in the middle of nowhere. The ground was very uneven and I'd taken the precaution of bringing a torch; I'd no intention of twisting my ankle.

'But Philpott completely took the wind out of my sails by saying, "We're just behind the Feathers, aren't we? I didn't know there were any houses here."

'I was dumbfounded. There I was, thinking I had him alone in the depths of the country, and it seemed the lane we were in ran parallel to one which had a pub in it. I hadn't even known there *was* a pub, but we'd finished up within a hundred yards of its back entrance.'

Ferris nodded, knowing the terrain. The Feathers could not be seen from the main road, and though there was a board proclaiming its whereabouts, it was quite feasible that Knowles had never noticed it.

'All I could do,' he was continuing, 'was make the best of the situation, so I stopped pretending and told him who I was and what I thought of him.

'He was a bit shaken at first, then he started to bluster. And the more he tried to justify himself, the angrier I got. Then he also lost his temper and shouted, "Anyway, why all the fuss? She brought it on herself; she'd been following me round for months, simply begging for it."

'That was it, really. I lashed out with my left and caught him on the chin. He went staggering backwards, then, recovering himself, started to run towards the pub, shouting over his shoulder that I was mad. There's not a proper access there, not much more than a gap in the hedge, but the grass was flattened, so it must be fairly well used.

'I went after him, because I was still determined to get compensation. I caught up with him just as he reached the gap and grabbed his arm, swinging him round, but he shook me off, laughing in my face.

' "God, the way you're carrying on, anyone would think you fancied her yourself! Is that what's eating you? Did I spoil a cosy little arrangement you had with your nympho sister?"'

Knowles broke off and leant forward, his head in his hands. The detectives didn't hurry him. Finally he looked up, his eyes bleary and inward-looking.

'I just—lost it. I'd forgotten I was still holding the torch, but suddenly I was bringing it down on his head with all the strength I could muster. And, not surprisingly, he went down.'

Knowles was breathing laboriously, as

268

though reliving his attack on Philpott. 'I waited for a minute to see if he'd get up, but he didn't. I couldn't leave him where he was, blocking the entrance, so I pulled him further into the car park, between two of the cars. I think I thought someone would find him before long, and give him any help he needed. I was damned if I was going to help him myself, but I swear to God it never occurred to me I'd killed him. I didn't find that out until the news broke the next day.'

He gave a short, bitter laugh. 'By merciful providence, I'd been wearing gloves; not for any sinister purpose, but simply because it was a bloody cold evening. Mind you, no one so much as approached me during the inquiry. Why should they? Philpott's public reputation worked against him, and his death was depicted, at least in the press, as a motiveless crime—an innocent man lured to his death, and not even robbed. Which, I need hardly say, suited me just fine.'

He reached for the glass of water in front of him and took a long drink. Webb didn't blame him. It was close in the small room, despite the high, open window, and the first rumbles of thunder could be heard in the distance.

Webb shifted on his seat. 'How did you feel when Judd's death was linked with Philpott's?'

Knowles shrugged. 'The similarity was a bit unnerving, and naturally I wasn't happy about the revival of interest in Philpott. Still, since

I'd had nothing whatever to do with Judd, I reasoned I wasn't in any more danger than I'd been before.'

'Until Mr Mace began airing his theories?' Webb asked, remembering Harry Good.

'That, I admit, put the fear of God into me. He'd really got his teeth into the case and he's an astute old so-and-so. I knew if he came up with anything, the police would take notice. They'd go back to Philpott's firm and start digging deeper.'

'So you tried to stop him?'

Knowles wasn't meeting his eye. 'I wasn't really thinking straight, but it seemed if I could just get hold of his notes, I'd have a clearer idea where I stood. But the desk drawer was locked and I couldn't break it, and I didn't dare hang around any longer.'

'So you waited outside till he walked his dog?' Webb persisted.

'I knew he took it out at nine-thirty every evening.'

Ferris leaned forward. '*How* did you know?'

Knowles flushed. 'His daughter mentioned it once.'

Webb wondered at the heightened colour, but didn't comment on it. 'Did she also mention the route?'

'Yes, she said whenever she took Goldie out, he wanted to go the way her father took him, down to the canal and home round the block.'

270

'So you were friendly with Mr Mace's daughter, but had no compunction about attempting to murder her father?'

This time, colour flooded his face. 'All right, Chief Inspector, you can't despise me any more than I do myself. I've no regrets about Philpott, but I'd give anything to take back what happened to old Frederick. Thank God he survived.

'In my defence, though you mightn't believe me, it was my mother and sister I was most worried about. My mother's dying and I couldn't let her find out everything right at the end like this.'

He looked up, beseechingly. 'Is there any way of keeping it quiet, just for a day or two?'

'I'm afraid not, sir, but if your mother's as ill as you say, it should be easy enough to keep it from her.'

'But I have to see her. I've been going in twice a day, and if I don't—'

'It's out of our hands, I'm afraid.'

And that, Webb thought, whatever sentence the court might impose, would be Knowles's real punishment.

*   *   *

'So it wasn't the assistant, after all?' Crombie commented, some days later.

'No; he *had* simply slipped and fallen, as his landlady said. What's more, it was just outside

271

the cinema, so there were plenty of witnesses, including,' Webb added meaningfully, 'a young lady who'd been to the cinema with him.'

'*Ah-hah!*'

'Quite so; he's not gay at all. That was simply uninformed gossip about a reserved young man who kept himself to himself.'

'Just goes to show,' said Crombie enigmatically.

*   *   *

If anything, Gillian was more concerned about Alex than Sonia. The latter was proving surprisingly strong; Mrs Knowles had died the day of Patrick's arrest, and Sonia had been left to deal with everything, including her distraught sister-in-law.

'Now that I know what was wrong with her, it's much easier to handle,' Sonia told her. 'Would you believe, neither Patrick nor Sybil had dared mention it to her in all this time? If I can get her to talk about it, I'm sure she'll be much better, and of course I can stress she's not the first or the last to have gone through this.

'Another thing, she's never worked since, just moped around the house all day being pampered by her mother, which gave her far too much time to think, and feel sorry for herself. I'm determined to ease her back into a job.'

Sonia'd smiled. 'This may all sound very altruistic, but I admit to an ulterior motive. I want her to have sufficient confidence to stay on in the cottage. It's not far away, after all, and when Patrick comes out of prison, I want to have him all to myself.'

Gillian suspected that this positive attitude came from the fact that Patrick was leaning on his wife so heavily, needing her now as he'd shown little sign of doing before.

Informed opinion was that his sentence on the murder charge might not be too severe, taking into account provocation and lack of premeditation—always providing his story was accepted. How he'd be dealt with regarding the attempted murder, Gillian didn't know, but she herself could never forgive him. It said a lot for the strength of her friendship with Sonia that it was surviving under such adverse conditions.

Alex, though, was another matter. Consumed as she was with guilt and horror, there was little Gillian could say to help her.

'And to think he tried to kill Pop, of all people—and that I unwittingly helped him! If I hadn't mentioned about Goldie—'

'—he'd simply have waited till Pop came out,' Gillian said firmly. 'It's no use torturing yourself like this, Alex. Anyway, thank God he's as good as new again.'

She studied her sister's downcast face. 'How do you explain all this heart-searching and remorse to Roy? He must have noticed it.'

'He's being very considerate,' Alex said quietly. 'I don't know how much he suspects; do you think I should tell him?'

'Not yet, and certainly not just to salve your conscience; that would do more harm than good. For all we know, the possibility of an affair might never have entered his head, and it would be pointless to hurt him unnecessarily.'

'I know you think I've been a fool,' Alex said, 'and you're right. But I'll make it up to him, I promise I will. I've learned my lesson.'

Which, Gillian acknowledged to herself, was at least something.

* * *

'Chief Inspector!' Edwina looked at Webb in surprise.

He smiled wryly. 'I suppose you thought you'd seen the last of me. This isn't an official visit, though.'

'It's nice to see you. Come through; we're in the garden.'

He followed her through the hall and large, homely kitchen and out of the back door. Frederick Mace, resplendent in a Panama hat, was seated in a deck chair under an apple tree.

'Good to see you home again, sir,' Webb greeted him, taking the hand the old man held out.

'Thank you. Sit down, sit down—Edwina's bringing out some lemonade. Yes, I had a lucky escape. It's hard to believe Sonia's chap was behind it. I never really took to him— didn't think he was good enough for her—but I never suspected he was a killer.' Mace shook his head sadly.

'So even you aren't infallible!' Webb commented.

The old man smiled. '*Touché*, Chief Inspector.' He paused, shooting Webb a calculating look from his keen grey eyes.

'Am I right in thinking you had your sights set on Paul Blake?'

'So much for my subtle approach! Only in passing, really, but I noticed you seemed surprised to hear he'd lived in Oxbury.'

'So I was, till I thought about it, but there'd really been no reason to mention it. He left before the murder, and in any case we never discussed his personal life. That, at least, has been rectified to some extent.'

'Oh?'

Mace ignored the implied question. 'Was that your only reason for suspecting him, apart from the size of his feet?'

Webb hesitated. 'Not quite, sir. I suspected—quite wrongly, as it turned out— that he might have been gay.'

Frederick Mace leant back in his chair. 'Now that *is* interesting. Why was that?'

'Just an off-the-cuff remark by his parents'

next-door neighbour.' Webb paused. 'Why is it interesting?'

Mrs Mace had rejoined them, and her husband waited while she passed round the glasses of lemonade and seated herself. Then he settled back in his chair.

'You know, of course, that along with Philpott's womanizing, I passed on the information that he had strong prejudices against homosexuals?'

Webb nodded.

'Well, I didn't put too much emphasis on it at the time; I was too busy congratulating myself that my suspicions of his being a ladies' man had been confirmed. However, when we left the Bradburns and I decided to go straight on to Oxbury, Paul did his best to dissuade me. I thought it was the long drive he was objecting to, but the following week he visited me in hospital, and when I suggested he went back there, he refused point-blank—said he couldn't fit it in, or some such excuse.

'I was astonished; he'd always agreed to my requests before, and I didn't know what to make of it. We parted, I'm afraid, on rather strained terms. To my relief, though, he returned later that day, saying he wanted to set the matter straight, but before he could do so, you arrived on the scene.'

'And waded in with my size elevens,' Webb said ruefully. 'Which, of course, ruffled him even more, but when you'd gone, I got the full story. It seems that although Paul was never homosexual, one of his friends was. This Charles had been at school with him, where he'd repeatedly stuck up for Paul when he was bullied, and the friendship—totally platonic, of course—had continued afterwards.

'What really is amazing, though, is that it was Paul and Charles whom Philpott insulted that evening at the cricket club. Paul says he was completely poleaxed when Mrs Bradburn mentioned it. He'd forgotten the incident—he was used to that kind of thing when he was out with Charles and had trained himself to ignore it. But what totally stunned him was that he'd had no idea until then that the man involved had been Trevor Philpott.

'It knocked him sideways, and he nearly blurted the whole thing out to me over lunch afterwards. God knows why he didn't, but during the next few days he got in more and more of a panic, realizing he now had what might appear to be a personal grudge against Philpott. So he decided to keep as far away from previous haunts as possible.

'He told me that after the visit to Mrs Bradburn he'd had another look at Philpott's picture, but even then he couldn't recognize him. It had been dark in the clubhouse, and as soon as Philpott started abusing them, Paul had turned away, refusing to meet his eye.

'So there you are, Chief Inspector.

Although you were wrong in your suspicions, there was a grain of truth buried there.'

Webb nodded, glad of the explanation. In view of his innocence, Blake's behaviour at the hospital had continued to puzzle him, and he didn't like to leave loose ends.

'Thank you very much for telling me, sir. So that's that, then. I must say, when this book of yours comes out, I'll be first in line to buy it. As a matter of interest, will you still include the Feathers case?'

'Most certainly I shall; you don't imagine I'd let all that work, not to mention a cracked head, go for nothing?'

'And the relevant Commandment, I suppose, was adultery?'

'Of course; Philpott was married, even if the girl wasn't. He'd been consistently unfaithful, and it finally caught up with him.'

'It'll make interesting reading. In the meantime'—Webb retrieved the paper bag from the grass beside him—'I wonder if you'd be kind enough to autograph *The Muddied Pool*? I found it fascinating.'

'How kind. I'd be delighted.'

Webb watched as he wrote a short dedication in his neat hand, and signed it with a flourish.

'Thank you. Well, it's been a pleasure to meet you, sir, and I wish your books every success. All the same, it might be safer not to include any unsolved crimes in future.'

'Don't worry, Chief Inspector,' Edwina assured him, 'I shall personally see to that.'

We hope you have enjoyed this Large Print book. Other Chivers Press or Thorndike Press Large Print books are available at your library or directly from the publishers.

For more information about current and forthcoming titles, please call or write, without obligation, to:

Chivers Press Limited
Windsor Bridge Road
Bath BA2 3AX
England
Tel. (01225) 335336

OR

Thorndike Press
P.O. Box 159
Thorndike, Maine 04986
USA
Tel. (800) 223-2336

All our Large Print titles are designed for easy reading, and all our books are made to last.